Would he [...] if he knew her secret?

"I'm sorry I've been so bitchy, Marc," Kyla sighed, leaning against his solid comforting chest.

He held her close. "You haven't been, darling. What's the matter? Feeling trapped?"

She shook her head. "I'm just...not used to the idea yet. I didn't think I'd ever get engaged—or married."

"That's silly and you know it," he replied softly. As his lips probed hers Kyla's senses reacted immediately, as usual. Marc was so wonderful, so different from other men. Surely she should make a clean breast of everything....

With an inner thud she descended from the sensuous cloud she'd been floating on. She *couldn't* tell Marc! She was too afraid of losing him....

DAPHNE CLAIR

the loving trap

Harlequin Books

TORONTO • LONDON • LOS ANGELES • AMSTERDAM
SYDNEY • HAMBURG • PARIS • STOCKHOLM • ATHENS • TOKYO

Harlequin Presents edition published June 1982
ISBN 0-373-10506-1

Original hardcover edition published in 1980
by Mills & Boon Limited

CHAPTER ONE

THE atmosphere in the spacious office was tense. In spite of the air-conditioning, Kyla felt sweat on the palms of her hands as she clasped them tightly in her lap, and pressed her knees together to stop them from visibly trembling under the skirt of her sophisticated silk-look dress. She looked graceful and cool and stylish in clear green that matched the colour of her eyes, her long dark brown hair drawn back neatly from symmetrical features, giving her an air of aloofness that successfully hid the nervous strain she knew she must not show.

Her eyes skimmed from the man sitting behind a desk big enough for table-tennis, to light with relief on the park beyond the first-floor window, where children raced about with the unquenchable energy of the very young, and their mothers sat thankfully in the shade of pepper trees and willows, away from the scorching heat of the sun. A council gardener, stripped to the waist, was weeding around the brilliant flower beds.

'*Miss Vernon!*'

Clearly exasperated, Marc Nathan's hard male voice called her to the business in hand. Her softly feminine mouth tightened instinctively as she returned her green gaze to the dark, angry stare of gunmetal grey he was directing at her. He said with slow, insulting distinctness, 'That *is* my final offer.'

'I heard you the first time, Mr Nathan,' Kyla said.

'Well?' The query was peremptory. There was a frown between his dark brows and a tightness about the muscles of his face. His strong will was showing, and for a moment she felt cowed inwardly. She quickly pulled herself together, more than ever determined not to show a sign of intimidation. Her eyes flashed angry defiance, and the third person in the room hastily intervened as she took a sharp breath, preparing to tell the arrogant head of Nathan & Signet just what he could do with his offer, his plans for expansion, and himself.

'Why don't you think it over, Miss Vernon?' Bernard King suggested quietly.

Kyla hesitated, her eyes swinging to the lawyer, and he added persuasively, 'It's a very good offer, you know. I suggest you contact your own lawyer and talk it over with him. I'm sure——' he cast a look that might have held a warning at Marc Nathan '—I'm sure that Mr Nathan will allow you a few days to decide.'

Mr Nathan looked as though he wanted to say something explosive. His right hand made a powerful-looking fist on the mahogany top of the desk, and his jaw looked ominously set, but he said nothing.

Taking silence for consent, Bernard King turned to Kyla. 'Shall we say, until Friday? And I do urge you most strongly to get legal advice, before making a final decision.'

'I have had legal advice,' Kyla said clearly. 'And I have every right to remain in my shop until the lease runs out five years from now.'

'Yes, of course,' the lawyer said, ignoring a suppressed sound of irritation from the man behind the big desk. 'But I really meant that you should take advice as to your best interests, as well as your rights.'

'We did suggest,' the other man reminded her with barely masked impatience, 'that you should ask your legal adviser to attend this meeting with you.'

'Yes, I know you did, Mr Nathan,' Kyla answered coolly. 'But it *was* a suggestion, wasn't it—not an order?'

For an instant she thought there was a gleam of reluctant

amusement in the hostile darkness of his eyes. Then he said grimly, 'I'm well aware, Miss Vernon, that I don't have the right to give you orders.'

His tone implied that he would have relished having that right, and the antagonism she felt deepened and became even sharper.

Something must have shown in her face despite her effort to remain calm and unruffled. The gunmetal gaze trained on her suddenly narrowed, and something within her trembled.

She had a desperate urge to escape. Although the office was spacious, and artificially cooled, it gave her an overwhelming impression of closeness that was almost claustrophobic.

She rose quickly to her feet. On the thick carpet her high-heeled sandals felt unsafe, but she managed to stand straight as she said, looking at the older man, 'Very well, Mr King. If you insist, I will give you my final answer on Friday. But I should warn you that nothing you or Mr Nathan has said today makes the slightest difference. I don't want to move, and I have no intention of doing so. Goodbye, Mr Nathan,' she added, her eyes skimming the desk before she turned to the door the lawyer was opening for her.

Marc Nathan didn't say goodbye, but he got to his feet and gave her a brief nod as she left the room. Kyla wondered where he had learned such good manners.

The door closed behind her, and in the empty corridor she sagged against the jamb for a few moments with the release of the tension that had gripped her for the past half-hour. Through the wood of the door she heard Marc Nathan also relieving his feelings in a harsh outburst. His voice came to her quite clearly, demanding, 'What the hell is the matter with the bloody little fool? Does she think I'll go higher than that? She's already been offered twice what her junky little business is worth!'

Well, thank you, Mr Nathan! thought Kyla as she moved away down the corridor and passed the girl at the desk in the outer office with a weary smile.

She walked down the stairs rather than wait for the lift, and went along the street a few doors to her *junky little shop*.

She thought herself it was a rather nice little shop, and although she was not in the million-dollar profit bracket that she suspected was Marc Nathan's natural habitat, she made a good living from it. In fact, before Nathans had taken over the building and begun persuading the tenants to give up their leases and move elsewhere on the compensation paid out to them, she had been considering a modest expansion of her own. The barber next door was elderly and unwell, and on the point of retirement. She had hoped to take over his lease and use the extra space for her second-hand stock, giving her more room to display the handcrafts and books that made up the bulk of her business. But Nathans wanted to pull down the old building and erect a modern office block on the site, and old Mr Birch had been pleased enough to accept a substantial cash payment for the remainder of his lease. Most of the other tenants, too, had been quite amenable. Some had gone into premises nearer the main street that were larger and more modern than the small, outdated shops in the old Fisher Building, and they were pleased with their move. Only Kyla had been reluctant. And as the pressure on her increased, she became militant. She was entitled to see out her lease, and that was what she intended to do.

So big business, in the shape of Nathans and its Managing Director, was being inconvenienced, she thought—too bad. *Her* customers, with their modest spending power, were people too, she mentally told Mr Nathan. They liked coming to her attractive little shop in its quiet side-street next to the park, with the bus stop just around the corner, and the car park not far away. And their convenience was important to her livelihood.

She touched her fingers to her own hand-lettered name on the window in which she had arranged a display of pottery, and turned into the shady doorway.

Hazel Wright, the pleasant, middle-aged woman who was her part-time assistant, glanced up from where she was pricing some baby clothes that had come in for the swop shop, as they tended to call their second-hand clothing corner. Some customers never brought money at all, but offered something saleable of their own in return for their purchases.

Hazel smiled, pushing a curl of pepper-and-salt hair from over her blue eyes, and asked, 'Well, how did it go?'

'Deadlock,' Kyla said succinctly. Coming round the counter she began to look over the tiny garments on the top. 'These are the things Mrs Arahopo brought in this morning, aren't they?' she asked. She hoped Hazel was not going to insist on a complete rundown of the meeting.

Hazel glanced at her with a slightly resigned smile. 'That's right. She said her mother did most of the knitting. It's very good. What about asking her if she's willing to make some things for the new stock?'

Grateful for Hazel's easy acceptance of the fact that she didn't want to talk about her discussion with the head of Nathan & Signet, Kyla replied, 'That sounds like a good idea. I'll talk to Mrs Arahopo next time she comes in and ask her what she thinks of it.'

For the rest of the afternoon, Kyla tried to forget the interview with Marc Nathan. A party of American tourists wandered in just before closing time, after Hazel had gone home and left Kyla on her own. The tourists were looking for genuine New Zealand souvenirs to take home with them, and Kyla showed them carved kauri spoons with

Maori motifs, inlay work in paua shell and some handsome tooled leatherwork. One woman bought a set of leather drink coasters and a kauri bowl and spoon. Another poked about in a dissatisfied way and asked if there wasn't something a bit more colourful like a teatowel, or maybe a scarf, or something like that.

Kyla suggested she try the souvenir shop that was around the corner, wrapped the other buyer's purchases and kept smiling until they had regained the street and she was able to close the door behind them and turn the *Closed* sign against the glass.

She glanced at the clock and saw that it was well after five. Chris Cameron would be waiting for her in the car park at the rear of the buildings. Her own car was being repaired, and Chris had offered to pick her up after work and take her home. She had told him she would meet him at the car, not to call for her. Chris worked for Nathans in their sales department, and she knew that although he tried not to show it, he was a little nervous of being identified with the young woman who was causing such frustration to his boss.

Her relationship with Chris was ambiguous. Hazel called him her boy-friend, a word Kyla disliked. Yet he was more than an ordinary friend, she supposed. Certainly he would have liked their association to be closer than it was, but one reason she liked him so much was that he seemed prepared to let her set the pace. He was undemanding enough for her to feel secure in his company, and he was, she admitted with a slightly guilty twinge, useful for those occasions when a girl was expected to arrive with a male escort, and for her social life generally.

Automatically, before she left, she checked her appearance in the mirror at the rear of the shop. Her dress was still clean and uncreased, her hair smooth, her light make-up faultlessly applied. Reassured, she knew that this was how Marc Nathan had seen her—the outward poise and assurance, the crisp, businesslike manner that hid the flutter of nerves in her stomach and the inward trembling when she stood up to him.

She told herself there was nothing personal in her antagonism to Mr Nathan. It was what he stood for that she was fighting, the power of big corporations over smaller business people, the assumption that a rich firm like Nathans had some sort of right to override the interests of people with low spending levels, like many of her customers.

But she did dislike big, aggressive men, and in spite of his well-groomed appearance, the neat cutting of his dark, thick hair, the crisp collared shirt and smart business suit, Marc Nathan's forceful personality showed in every incisive gesture he made, in the firmly moulded mouth, the hard, calculating eyes, the deep, assertive voice.

She had seen him, long before she ever spoke to him, striding across the car park with one hand casually thrust into a pocket of his trousers, his air of blatant male assurance even then causing a faint prickle of antipathy down her spine. She couldn't help knowing who he was; the Nathan & Signet executives had labelled reserved spaces for their cars in the parking area. He drove a smaller car now than when she had first opened her shop two years ago, but the new car was just as classy in its way, a lowslung two-seater of Japanese make. Mr Nathan evidently was not a family man, or else he left the family car for his wife to use, she had thought. But Chris had told her that his boss was a loner. It fitted. She couldn't really imagine him surrounded by a loving family of children.

Oh, yes, she knew who Marc Nathan was; sometimes she watched him get into his shiny maroon car, hovering behind the small back window beside the rear door of the shop until he had turned and driven away, before emerging herself to enter her own much more unobtrusive vehicle. Mr Nathan obviously hadn't known that she existed until she replied to the letter from his solicitors, intimating that she was refusing to surrender her lease. There had been one more letter and a similar reply before she looked up one day from serving a customer and found that Marc Nathan was the reason for the sudden blocking of the light from the doorway.

He stood there for a moment, giving the whole shop a swift, silent appraisal before he moved inside. Kyla wrenched her attention from him and back to her customer, but all the while she was helping the young woman decide between a hand-painted smock top and a drawn-thread embroidered blouse, she was conscious of the man in the background looking over the shelves of pottery, wood-ware and novelty crafts, dodging a macramé plant-holder that hung from a ceiling beam, and lifting a dark eyebrow as he gave a cursory glance at the racks and shelves of used clothing in the swop shop corner.

The young woman left and a Maori mother passed her in the doorway, parking a pushchair inside the door to one side and lifting a wriggling child from it while another clutched at her skirt. Tempted to ignore the tall man now coming towards the counter in favour of the new customer, she saw the young mother was making for the second-hand clothing. Marc Nathan stood before her, saying, 'Miss Vernon?' in peremptory tones.

'Yes——?' answered Kyla, a hint of enquiry in her own voice, and not a vestige of recognition allowed to show in her face.

He looked at her in a measuring way, then said, 'I'm Marc Nathan.'

'I know,' she said calmly.

A brief flicker of something—surprise or amusement, perhaps—gleamed for an instant in his eyes, and he said,

'Is there somewhere we can talk in private?'

There was only a curtained cubbyhole where she had a small desk for doing accounts and a tiny sink and bench for making tea.

Kyla shook her head. 'I'm sorry,' she said. 'In any case, I have customers to attend to.' Two more people had just entered and were peering at the price tags on some batik caftans just inside the door. One of them moved to the book display and began leafing through a volume of photographs of early Northland. He was a thin young man with a beard, and he handled the book with care, as Kyla saw in a quick glance. The girl who had come in with him took one of the caftans down and held it against her slight body, as Marc Nathan was saying, 'I would like to talk to you, Miss Vernon——'

The girl looked up, catching her eye, and Kyla said, 'Excuse me, Mr Nathan,' and went over to the girl, asking if she wanted to try on the caftan and directing her to the curtained corner which served as a changing room.

When she returned to the counter the young man was there, the book on the counter top, his hand digging in his back pocket, pulling out some notes to pay for his purchase. 'We're new in Whangarei,' he told her as she wrapped the book. 'Do you have any maps of the city and the district?'

'I have a guidebook to Northland which has maps incorporated,' she told him. 'But for maps on their own, try stationery shops. There are two not very far from here.'

She showed him the guidebook, told him how to find the stationers and added directions to the Information Centre in town. The girl came out with the caftan over her arm, saying regretfully that she didn't think it looked quite right. 'Sorry,' she added as Kyla returned it to its hanger.

'That's all right,' Kyla smiled. And as they left, thanking her, she added, 'Come in again.'

They would, they assured her, and she believed them. They were the kind of people who formed some of her most regular customers, and they had obviously liked the shop.

Marc Nathan was still standing before the counter, his hands thrust deep into his pockets, feet apart as though he was balancing on his heels. But before she could get back to him, the young mother, who had been trying clothes on her wriggling offspring all the while, called her over to ask the price of a jersey which had somehow lost its tag. Kyla looked at the woman's cheap, worn cotton frock, the neatly mended tear in the baby's flowered tee-shirt and the outgrown jeans the other child wore, and gave her a price that was certainly much lower than whatever had been written on the lost tag. The woman beamed and gathered up a pile of clothing which she handed to Kyla to be wrapped, the jersey on top. It was a pretty pink, an angora knit, and would look fantastic with the baby's warmly brown skin. To Kyla's mind it didn't matter in the least that the baby was a boy.

The woman paid and left, chattering and laughing with the toddler who helped to push the baby in his chair, and Marc Nathan turned to Kyla and said, 'She took the label off, herself, you know. I saw her.'

He didn't miss much, then, thought Kyla. She said evenly, 'Thank you, Mr Nathan. I'll run my business my own way.'

'I was offering information,' he said, 'not advice.'

'Then thank you for the information. What did you want to see me about?'

'You don't need three guesses,' he said drily. Then, as another couple came in, he frowned in annoyance and asked, 'Don't you have an assistant or something? Can't you leave someone else in charge for a while—we can't talk here.'

'My assisant is part-time,' she told him. 'She isn't here at the moment. And as I presume it's about my lease, I'm afraid you're wasting your time, anyway. And mine. As you can see, I'm rather busy, and I've told your lawyers twice that I don't want to relinquish the lease.'

'Look, be reasonable,' he said. 'All the other tenants have accepted our terms.'

'That's their business, Mr Nathan. This is mine.'

'We're offering very generous compensation, you know——'

'That isn't enough,' she cried crisply, about to add something to the effect that money couldn't buy everything.

But he straightened suddenly, taking his hands from his pockets and saying cuttingly, 'I see. Well, you're a businesswoman, Miss Vernon, I'll give you that. You have something that you know we want very much, and you're going to stick out for the best price you can get. You know, I thought that woman might have put one over you. But maybe the garment was over-priced in the first place, so when she thought she was getting a bargain she was only paying a realistic price, after all. You'll be hearing from our solicitors again. Good day.'

She heard from them, offering her more money. Tired of answering their letters, she threw this one away, tearing it with great satisfaction into half a dozen pieces and screwing it up savagely before putting it into the wastebasket in her tiny 'office'.

Then they phoned her. Had she received their letter? Mr King wanted to know. Yes? Well, had she considered their offer? Did she realise that it was an extremely high offer—a considerable sum of money, which would surely enable her to acquire much more desirable premises elsewhere in the city? Mr King plainly could not understand why she simply reiterated that she preferred the present site of her shop to any other, and intended to stand by her legal right to remain there.

Mr King rang off, perplexed, and the next letter she received suggested a meeting between herself and Mr Nathan and their respective legal representatives. Kyla supposed ignoring it would only bring another telephone call, so she reluctantly agreed. Perhaps if she nerved herself to tell the man to his face that she was not interested in any amount of compensation, they would stop bothering her.

Well, she had not quite done that—at least, she had, but he had raised his offer to a sum which had made her suppress a gasp, and which clearly his own legal adviser had not approved of, judging by Mr King's worried glance when he had made it. And then she had allowed herself to be persuaded to take more time.

She opened the back door and paused a moment, looking about the shop. She really did need more room. The fact that she could no longer have the shop next door was going to be a serious drawback. But where else would she find such a good site for the type of clientele that she had? If she moved to a newer place on the main street, the character of the shop would change, her clientele would be different. She might, she admitted, make more money, but what she had was more than sufficient for her modest needs, and the satisfaction would be considerably less, she felt. That was something that Marc Nathan, running a million-dollar business from his elegant decorator-designed office in the three-storey Nathan building, would never be able to understand.

She locked the door behind her, realising guiltily that she must have kept Chris waiting, and began to hurry along the narrow footpath at the rear of the shops, searching with her eyes for Chris's Cortina among the cars still parked in the large tarsealed area.

The car park was surrounded by buildings, and there were surprisingly few people about for this time of the day. A woman hurried two children into a car and backed out hastily, followed by one of the Nathans executives in a big American car. Three young men in leather jackets and torn jeans sat chatting astride their powerful motorcycles near the footpath, and as Kyla neared them, one turned to watch her, then ambled over to stand blocking her way.

As she halted, he stood looking her over insolently, his jaws moving on a wad of chewing gum, thumbs stuck into a tooled leather belt.

Frigidly, Kyla said, 'Excuse me, please.'

The man grinned, and his two friends came to their feet, watching. Kyla saw a movement in the centre of the car park, and caught a glimpse of Chris's fair head as he got out of his car. Encouraged, she said firmly, 'Let me past, please. Someone is waiting for me.'

'Like a ride?' the man asked. One of the others laughed and said something she didn't catch, but the three of them seemed to find it funny.

'No, thanks.' She shook her head, glancing over to where Chris had parked his car. She saw him take one step and then stop, hesitating. The man in front of her was grinning, and the other two moved closer, one coming to join his friend, and other moving beside and behind her. She stepped back, and hearing footsteps behind her, jerked her head to look over her shoulder.

A hard arm came about her waist and her head collided softly with a jacket lapel over a broad chest. Marc Nathan's deep voice said pleasantly, 'The lady is with me, boys.'

His hand on her waist urged her ruthlessly forward, and the two in front simply parted, hunching their shoulders, and let him guide her on down the path, until they reached his car. He unlocked the passenger door, and Kyla protested, 'But—I can't——'

'Don't make a liar of me,' he said. 'They're watching.'

Then Chris came hurrying up, his face flushed. 'My car's over there, Kyla,' he said. 'I was waiting for you.'

She looked at him as though she had never seen him before, and Marc Nathan said, 'I'm taking Miss Vernon home.'

He had the door open, and Kyla, suddenly discovering that she was trembling, sank into the passenger seat under the insistence of firm hands.

She heard Chris say unhappily, 'Are you all right, Kyla?'

She just managed to say, 'Yes,' before Marc Nathan said, 'I'll look after her,' and firmly closed the door. Moments later he was sliding into the car beside her, starting it immediately to glide out from the parking space while Chris stood uncertainly by, then returned to his own car with his head down.

As the car paused at the exit, Marc Nathan glanced at her and said, 'Do up your safety belt.'

It was a reel belt, easy enough to fasten, but Kyla's hands were shaking and she fumbled; the belt slipped from her fingers and slid back into its housing.

The man beside her directed a sharp glance at her face and leaned over to pull the belt down across her shoulder and snap it into place. The action brought him close to her, and Kyla instinctively pressed her spine back against the well-padded leather seat back. He gave her another quick, frowning glance and moved back behind the steering wheel.

As the car moved out into the flow of traffic she said, 'You don't need to take me home. I can get a bus if you just drop me round the corner.'

He cast her a glance that seemed scornful and said, 'Just tell me where you live.'

She obeyed briefly, and he said, 'Right, I know the street. What's happened to your car this week?'

'How do you know I have one?' she asked.

That earned her another of those looks. 'I've seen it in the car park. But not for the last couple of days.'

'It's being repaired,' she said. He had surprised her, but she supposed there was nothing significant about his having noticed which car was hers. She knew *his*, after all.

His next question startled her even more. He asked, 'Are you and Chris Cameron close?'

'No,' she said, caught unawares. 'We're friends.' Then, suddenly hostile, she added, 'Is that your business?'

'He seemed to expect you to go with him. I just wondered if I was butting in on anything.'

'Would you care?' she asked. Then immediately she added, 'I'm sorry, you've been kind and I didn't mean to be rude. Chris had arranged to give me a lift home tonight.'

Her hands were tightly clasped over the strap of the shoulder bag she held on her knee, and her voice sounded breathless and unsteady. He shifted into another traffic lane, passed through a green light and speeded up, drawing away from the business area to where the road was lined with houses on quarter-acre sections, neat modern homes with incipient gardens interspersed with old villas shaded by big mature trees.

Suddenly a firm hand reached out and briefly covered hers. 'Relax,' he said. 'They were only stupid kids, you know. There were too many people about for you to have come to any harm. They were just trying it on to see if they could frighten you.'

'Yes,' she said stiffly. 'Well, they did.'

His glance was a little puzzled. 'I know,' he said soberly.

Kyla looked out of her window at passing trees and houses, seeing gardens full of summer flowers, the occasional blaze of a coral tree and the brilliant splash of bougainvillaea backgrounded by the bush-covered hills that lay behind the city.

He turned into the quiet, sloping street where she lived, and she told him, 'It's the block of flats at the end.'

He drew up outside the low brick building, and critically surveyed the young birch tree on the small lawn at the front, and the four letterboxes at the entrance to the driveway.

Kyla made to get out, but the door catch was cunningly hidden under the armrest, and by the time she found it he was already on the pavement, opening her door from the outside.

She started to thank him, but he put a firm hand on her arm just above the elbow and asked, 'Which flat?'

'Three. But I'm quite all right now. I don't need——'

But he was not easily deterred. He came with her to the door, and when she took her key out of her bag he stood watching. She had been keeping herself tightly controlled for too long, and now the sight of her own front door must have triggered a reaction mechanism. She began shaking again, and when she fumbled with the key at the lock, the man watching with frowning eyes made an impatient, low sound, took the key from her and opened the door himself, almost shoving her inside as he closed it behind them both. The door opened straight into her small living room, and he pushed her into an armchair, saying, 'Sit down before you faint,' and, taking her bag from her, placed it on a small table beside the chair.

'I won't faint,' she said stubbornly.

'I wouldn't like to guarantee it. You're remarkably pale. Where do you keep your drinks?'

'What?' she said, vaguely indignant.

'You need a stiff brandy or whisky,' he explained patiently. 'For medicinal purposes. Or don't you keep alcohol about?'

'Not really,' she confessed. 'Only a bottle of sherry in the kitchen, in the cupboard by the stove.'

As he glanced around, found the doorway leading to the kitchen and strode purposefully towards it, she said feebly, 'But I don't need——'

He was already there, and half a minute later returned with a glass half full of sherry. He put it in her hand and as she held it, still a little rebellious, he said, 'Go on— drink it up. It will do you good.'

Kyla glanced up, decided that if she didn't he was probably capable of making her do it, and sipped the sherry down. He stood silently by, took the empty glass from her hand when she had finished and placed it beside her bag on the table.

'Better?' he queried.

'Thank you. Would you like some?'

He looked faintly amused. 'No, thanks.'

Kyla supposed his preferences didn't include cheap sherry. She had bought it for cooking, really. She was no connoisseur—not even a drinker.

She wished he wouldn't stand over her as he was doing, and as though he read the thought he moved away and sat down in another chair, looking at her critically. 'You've a bit more colour,' he remarked.

Embarrassed, she made to move out of the chair, wanting to give him a hint that she would prefer him to leave, but his voice stayed her. 'Don't move yet,' he advised. 'Try to relax.'

It was an impossibility with him in the room, but she didn't say so. She turned her head a little away from him and closed her eyes. Then she heard him move and her eyes immediately flew open, wide and apprehensive.

Standing in front of his chair, he frowned. 'You *are* nervous,' he said. 'I'll make you a cup of tea.'

She didn't even bother to argue this time. He would do as he liked anyway, so there was no sense in fighting him.

The tea was hot and he had sugared it, but asked her if

she wanted milk and poured it in last. He had not made
any for himself, but she was sure he was quite capable of
doing so without invitation if he wanted any, so she didn't
bother asking.

As she sipped at it, he said, 'You surprise me. I had you
down as a very cool lady. I would have thought you could
wipe the floor with those louts any time.'

'Three of them?' she said ironically. 'Wonder Woman
I'm not, Mr Nathan!'

'I hardly expected you to knock their heads together,'
he said. 'But if you'd shown them some of the determina-
tion that you demonstrated today in my office, they would
very likely have backed down.'

'Are *you* going to back down, Mr Nathan?' she challenged him.

'No. The two cases are not really the same, are they?' he
admitted.

'That's right, they're not. And you needn't think that
because I went to pieces over this, you'll find me easy to
bully in matters of business.'

His face grim, he said, 'I'm not a bully, Miss Vernon.
No threats have been made to you.'

No, they hadn't, she had to concede. But the very size
of Nathans was a threat in itself, just as Marc Nathan's
presence in the same room gave her a strong feeling of
nervous unease. He was too big, too sure of himself, too
blatantly masculine altogether, for comfort.

She drank the remainder of her tea quickly and put
down the cup.

'Are you nervous of being alone?' he asked her.

Kyla shook her head. She was far more so with him
sitting there only a few feet away, but he had been so
thoughtful she could hardly say so.

'I'm quite all right now,' she told him firmly, standing

up to prove it. 'You've been very kind, Mr Nathan. I don't know how to thank you.'

Coming to his feet too, he said, his grey eyes rather speculative, 'There is a way, if you're willing.'

Kyla recoiled—she couldn't help it.

'Good lord!' he snapped irritably, 'I didn't mean that! What do you take me for?'

She shook her head. 'I didn't—you misunderstood——'

'Did I?' he said sarcastically. 'What I was going to suggest was that you might have dinner with me tomorrow night—or any other night this week.' As she looked at him, wary and puzzled, he added on a very dry note, 'To discuss a certain matter of business which concerns us both. And I promise not to bully you.'

'You'll be wasting your time,' she warned him. 'And money.'

'You put a low value on your company.'

'You said it was business.'

'Combined with pleasure. I often find that a friendly talk over a good meal can help to iron out certain problems.'

'The tax-deductible business lunch?' Kyla murmured.

'That's right. Only in this case I'm talking dinner. Will you come—or would it violate your principles?'

'What would you know about my principles, Mr Nathan?'

'You might like to explain them to me over dinner tomorrow night. I have a feeling they include disapproval of expense account meals. Will it help if I say I don't intend to charge it to the firm?'

Kyla shrugged. 'That's your affair, Mr Nathan.' As he remained silently waiting, she said, 'I'll come. Thank you.'

'Good. Will seven o'clock suit you? I'll pick you up.'

'At the shop,' she said. 'I have things to do after closing time, and I can freshen up and change there.'

'I could bring you home first, if you like.'

'No, thank you.'

'Okay, if you're sure. At the shop, then. See you to-morrow.'

She closed the door behind him with relief, wondering how she had managed to get herself talked into *that*. A dinner date with Marc Nathan—the very thought of it threw her into a panic.

Calm down! she told herself. It was only business after all, and so far she had coped very adequately with the pressure Nathans had put on her. The man himself had said he had put her down as a very cool lady. The image must have been shaken more than a little by her behaviour this afternoon, but she had more than twenty-four hours to recover her equilibrium and present him tomorrow night with the competent, assured manner that had been carefully cultivated and which seldom slipped as badly as it had today.

CHAPTER TWO

CHRIS came into the shop the following morning, his look anxious and faintly embarrassed. He also seemed rather aggrieved that she had gone home the day before with Marc Nathan.

'I'd waited for you for nearly twenty minutes, you know,' he told her. 'We did have an arrangement, didn't we?'

'Yes,' said Kyla. 'I'm sorry, Chris. But I'd had a bit of a fright, and Mr Nathan sort of took over. He told them he was with me, and they were watching. It would have looked a bit odd if I'd gone off with you, after that.'

'It wouldn't have mattered what they thought, surely? I was on my way over, you know, when the boss put his oar in.'

Perhaps he had been coming, but she couldn't forget that last glimpse she had seen of him, stopping in his tracks as he took in the three men converging on her. It was unfair to blame him for hesitating; he was not a big man and his very lack of masculine aggression was the chief quality that had attracted her to him. But her faith in him had been undeniably shaken. Unfair or not, she couldn't help feeling that he should have come to the rescue more quickly.

She said, 'I was very grateful that Mr Nathan did put his oar in, as you call it.' As he flushed angrily she added, 'He was closer than you were, Chris, that's all.'

'Yes, well—how about tonight?' he said sulkily. 'Do I give you a lift?'

Kyla hesitated. 'I'm staying on at the shop for a while,' she said finally.

'I don't mind staying with you,' he said. 'How late will you be?'

'I'm going out for dinner later.'

He was surprised. 'Who with?' he demanded.

She might have told him it was not his business, but that seemed a rather futile thing to do. She had never had another date since Chris had first persuaded her to go out with him, and it seemed quite on the cards that some office grapevine would inform him that his boss had taken her out to dinner. For all she knew Marc Nathan had scrawled her name on a memo pad on that ostentatiously large desk of his, or asked his secretary to remind him that he had a business dinner with Kyla Vernon tonight. The secretary had probably made the reservations.

She said evenly, 'Actually, with your boss.'

'What?' He was thrown for a moment, then he said meaningly. 'Oh, I see. In return for services rendered. Quite the knight errant, isn't he?'

'Don't be silly!' Kyla said sharply. 'He wants to talk to me about the lease.'

'Oh, sure! He doesn't miss a trick, does he? He'll take you somewhere with music and candlelight and try to charm you into giving in to him.'

'Then he'll be disappointed,' said Kyla shortly. 'Excuse me, Chris, I have customers to see to.'

He was probably right about the tactics she might expect, she supposed. Marc Nathan could be gentle when he liked, and most women would probably appreciate his rather tough brand of good looks and his air of hard male assurance. Chris had hinted once that although he had no permanent ties, he was not averse to the company of women, and had been seen with some pretty glamorous ones in the past.

Chris's outline of the probable course the evening would take was fairly predictable, but her dinner companion was going to find that she was immune to that kind of persuasion.

He knocked on the door five minutes before seven, as she was inspecting her appearance in the customers' full-length mirror. She had chosen a cool silk dress in an unusual shade of grey-green that showed up her eyes as almost emerald by contrast. Thin straps crossed her tanned shoulders, the back was low and the bodice was gathered into soft folds over her nicely rounded breasts, and tied between them so that the material dipped a little—just enough to emphasise her womanly shape. The waist fitted snugly and the skirt was full and swirly, clinging on the hips and falling in folds to her calves, above slim ankles. Her legs were bare and smooth, and a pair of black high-heeled sandals showed off pretty feet. Her hair was in its usual neat coil, but she had adorned it with a silver filigree hair buckle, and taken a single narrow silver bracelet from stock to put on her right arm.

She had put on just a touch more make-up than usual, feeling a need to compete in some way with the girls Marc Nathan usually took out, to give her extra confidence. Her dark lashes looked longer than ever with a discreet coating of mascara, and she had shadowed her eyes with a soft green that came close to matching her dress, making them subtly luminous. A new, rather brighter lipstick than the one she normally wore completed the picture.

Satisfied with the poise and calm sophistication of the image that gazed back at her, she turned without haste to cross the floor of the shop and open the door.

Marc Nathan stepped in as she closed the door behind him, and turned immediately to look at her, so that she stayed standing just in front of it, because otherwise she would have had to walk round him.

Perhaps because he stood so close as his gaze slipped over her in a leisurely way, she found herself almost breathless with the force of his personality. He seemed to have shed the one that had been so much to the fore during their interview in his office, hard, driving and singleminded, and acquired a different one altogether.

It wasn't one that she liked any better, she told herself, stiffening instinctively under his undoubtedly appreciative, wholly masculine scrutiny. He stood casually, more relaxed than she had ever seen him, with one hand hooked into the belt of his trousers, pushing the jacket of his light-weight grey suit away from a taut waist. His head was a little to one side and he was smiling in a way that disturbed her. This was not the sharp-eyed, cold businessman she knew; it was a man prepared to enjoy an evening of plea-sure with a woman whom he blatantly found attractive, a man intent on ensuring that she realised to the full his own virile attraction for her sex.

'You look very nice,' he commented. Even his voice seemed different. There was no hardness in it now; it was a low, lazy drawl that went with his relaxed stance and the quite devastating smile that he directed at her.

'Thank you,' she managed to say, making the barest movement away from the door. He smiled at her a moment longer and then moved a little back so that she was able to walk past him, saying, 'I'm nearly ready. I'll get my bag.'

Kyla retreated behind the cubbyhole curtain, and found herself leaning against the small desk with her hands on it to support her, taking deep breaths to calm suddenly jump-ing nerves. She couldn't back out now; there was no excuse she could give. If she did, he would know that he could frighten her. And it was important that he didn't guess. In any case, she told herself sensibly, there was no logical reason for her fear. He was a civilised man, after all, re-spected in the community—a man who had come to her aid yesterday with every appearance of sympathy, and certainly with some chivalry. All he had done so far was look —and if she made it clear that she was not interested in the implications of that look, he would accept her refusal. For him there were plenty of other fish in the sea, and his self-image was probably too important to the man for him to risk a rebuff. She would be safe enough.

She pulled out her shoulder bag and transferred a small make-up sachet, a couple of tissues, a comb and some money into a small black beaded purse, pushing the shoulder bag into the deep drawer of the desk. The night was warm and humid and she really didn't need a wrap, but all the same she picked up a long black Indian silk scarf with jet-fringed ends and drew it round her shoulders with the ends crossed on the left one, so that it hid the bare flesh above the neckline of her dress.

When she emerged from behind the curtains she found her escort interestedly studying a book from the display rack. He looked up and then slowly returned the volume to its place, giving the racks a parting glance as he came over to her. 'You have some interesting stuff there,' he commented. 'Do you sell a lot of books?'

'Quite a number. I don't keep a large stock of each title, but I can order more if customers request them.'

'You don't have much fiction.'

'The range of fiction is so large I would scarcely know where to start. It's easily obtained elsewhere, so I tend to specialise in local writers, New Zealand art and nature books, and craft manuals. There's a shelf of paperback fiction in the swop shop, though—the second-hand section over there,' she explained as he looked askance.

'Second-hand, too?' he enquired, walking over to the section and running a long finger along the titles.

'Yes. Most of them wouldn't be to your taste, I think,' she said.

'Historical dramas and love stories?' he queried, putting his hand in his pocket as he turned from the shelf. 'Do many women read that junk?'

Kyla gave him a level glance. 'What do *you* read for relaxation, Mr Nathan? The *Encyclopædia Britannica*?'

His mouth quirked a little in acknowledgement of her sarcasm. 'Actually, I like a good thriller, and occasionally I read a Western. Which leaves me wide open, I suppose.'

'Yes, doesn't it?' Kyla agreed pleasantly. 'If your fantasies run to mayhem and murder and the occasional smoking six-gun, do you think you can afford to criticise women for preferring to read about romantic encounters with Regency gentlemen or desert sheiks? Surely theirs is a less harmful kind of fantasy than the violent kind that men seem to indulge in?'

'Okay!' He held up a hand in mock-surrender. 'Glass houses——! I won't throw another stone. All the same, I deny that I've been corrupted by James Bond. I really don't see myself as another 007!'

Remembering the spy's treatment of women, Kyla hoped not. Actually, she thought that Marc Nathan had enough character of his own to prohibit him feeling any need to adopt that of a fictional hero.

'By the way,' he said now, 'don't you think we might dispense with the formality, as this is at least partly a social occasion? My name is Marc—Kyla.'

She gave him a brief, cool look and said, 'All right, Marc,' with what she hoped was a convincingly casual air.

'Ready? Then let's go,' he said. 'I have a table booked for seven fifteen.'

The restaurant was licensed and cosy. The lighting was not by candles, but it was discreetly shaded and at least one or two couples obviously found it romantic.

Kyla refused a drink before the meal but allowed the waiter to pour some of the wine Marc had ordered into the stemmed glass before her, sipping it sparingly but with pleasure. They bypassed the tua-tua soup on the menu in deference to the heat of the evening, beginning with a delicious mixed seafood cocktail and following it with wild pork and a crisp salad for Kyla, and a carpetbag steak for Marc. She let him lead the conversation, and at first he confined it to the news headlines of the day, and a new TV programme that everyone seemed to be talking about. He listened to her opinions quietly and gave his own without heat. They didn't differ much, and he was better informed about international affairs than she was, so that she found herself listening with interest to what he had to say about the news from the Middle East and Europe.

Just as their main courses reached the table he introduced a more personal note. 'Where's your home town, Kyla?' he asked casually. 'You weren't born and bred in the North, were you?'

'Are you guessing?' she said lightly, hedging. 'Or can you tell a southerner when you see one?'

He smiled. 'Maybe. I have a theory, anyway, that Northlanders are more warm and friendly than people further south. It's our climate, perhaps.'

'So I'm cold and unfriendly?' she said.

'Cool and reserved, I would have said,' he countered swiftly. 'I wasn't getting at you.'

'Then I won't say what I was going to.'

'Which was?' he queried with obvious amusement. 'Come on, Kyla. If you didn't mean to tell me you shouldn't have piqued my curiosity with that teaser.'

She picked up her knife and fork, hesitated then said, 'I wouldn't have picked *you* for a Northlander, by that criterion.'

'You pack a punch, don't you?' he murmured, his eyes gleaming. 'First impressions are sometimes in error. We'll see what we can do about that, later.'

He picked up his glass and watched her over its rim as he sipped at the wine, before replacing it on the starched tablecloth. Alarmed, Kyla bent her head over her meal and tried to concentrate on that. He had not yet touched his, and felt his gaze on her as she resolutely swallowed the first mouthful of delicious tender pork. It was difficult, and she helped it down with a gulp of wine. 'You were born and bred here, weren't you?' she said, to break the silence.

'That's right,' he said, beginning at last to cut into his steak. 'My grandfather was a gumdigger. When he had saved a bit of money from that he married my grandmother and set up a little shop, selling kauri gum, and tools for the men in the gum-fields, on the corner where Nathan & Signet stands now.'

'On that actual corner?' queried Kyla, surprised. 'I didn't know that.'

'Yes, on that actual corner,' he confirmed. 'I have a photo of the old boy standing outside the place in shirt-sleeves and braces.'

'Do you look like him?'

'I don't know. He had a very full beard in the photo, and I don't remember him.'

'It's still a family business, isn't it?' Kyla asked.

'Not entirely, by any means. My father went into partnership with George Signet and they turned it into a wholesale business specialising in tools and machinery. My father died seven years ago, and George followed three years later.'

'Is that when you became head of the firm?'

'That's right. George had no children of his own, and after my father went, he groomed me to take over.

'So there's no Mr Signet, now?'

'No. Only Mr Nathan—third generation.'

She wondered if he intended to marry some day and provide a fourth generation to carry on the family name and business.

'What about your family, Kyla?' he asked. 'Do you have a father and mother somewhere south of Auckland?'

Kyla shrugged. 'My business has no family connections. The shop is all mine.'

'Not going to tell me about your family?' he insisted.

'You said this was business.'

'Combined with pleasure, I said. Where do you come from, Kyla?'

'South of Auckland, as you guessed. Why do you want to expand your building? Do you have some sort of compulsion to carry on where your father and Mr Signet left off?'

He noted her reluctance to talk about herself with a long, analytical stare before he replied. 'It isn't a psychological compulsion, if that's what you mean. The compulsion comes about because the business has grown a lot in the last few years. The market has expanded considerably, we have overseas contracts to fulfil and we need space for more operations. And obviously the logical place for that space is on the site right next door to our present offices and showrooms, which conveniently came up for sale at the right time.'

'But with tenants who don't want to move out. Did you think of them when you bought the building?'

Marc Nathan finished a mouthful of steak and took a sip from his wine-glass before he answered her. 'Of course we thought of them. We knew they would require reasonable compensation for surrendering their leases, and took that into account. It was a logical assumption that they would find themselves better off in the long run if they moved to better premises, and we made sure that they had the funds to do just that. And they have—with one exception.'

Kyla didn't answer, her head bent to her meal. Marc finished the wine in his glass and refilled it, making to top up her half full one. But Kyla stopped him, her fingers spread over the glass.

'This will be plenty for me, thanks,' she said.

'Keeping a clear head?' he asked. 'You needn't worry. Seduction isn't on the menu tonight.'

'I didn't suggest it was,' she said crisply. 'I never have more than one glass of wine, and I find a clear head a distinct advantage when I'm talking business.'

'Okay, let's talk business. I've told you why we need the site——'

'No, you haven't. You've told me why it would suit you to have it. And it suits me to stay right where I am. Apart from the fact that Nathans is a much bigger business, why should you be entitled to push me out of a site just because you happen to want it?'

He finished his steak and pushed his plate aside, looking at her with a wryly thoughtful expression. 'The building is old and your shop is cramped and out of the main stream of the shopping area. Why should you want to hold on to it so desperately?'

'We'll come to that later,' said Kyla, pushing her own plate away and clasping her hands on the table. 'I asked what gave you the right to try and push me out. You're not going to tell me it's for my own good?'

'Not as a primary motive, I admit. But if you see Nathans as the big bad wolf gobbling up little pigs, think again. We're not intent on squeezing you out of business or riding roughshod over the rights of the small shopkeeper. We want to make a deal—a fair deal. We help you into bigger and better premises, in return for your giving us room to build bigger and better premises for *our* operation. And your stubborn attitude is causing us more than inconvenience. We didn't spend peanuts buying that building, you know. If we can't build until your lease runs out it will mean a substantial financial loss, quite apart from the expense of finding another site that would not be nearly so suitable.'

'I'm sorry about that,' Kyla said calmly. 'But it was a risk you took, wasn't it?'

'Yes.' His tone was even, but the single syllable had a clipped-off sound as though he held on to his temper with some effort. 'There is also the fact that we have a thriving and expanding export market, which is important as a source of overseas funds for this country. The new building will help that along.'

'So it's my patriotic duty to help you make more money?' She laughed, and saw his lean jaw tense with temper.

'It's something the courts may well take into account,' he said.

'Courts?' Kyla's head lifted. 'You said you wouldn't threaten me.'

'I'm not threatening you. Surely you must realise that we can't just sit on an investment like that because one young woman won't see reason? If you don't move, of course we'll take it to court. And our advice is that we stand at least an even chance of winning. If it can be shown that your refusal of our terms is malicious or unreasonable.'

'You're bluffing!' she accused him. 'My lawyer told me I have a legal right to see out my lease.'

'In general terms, yes. But if—if it comes to a legal wrangle, Kyla, we can retain the best legal advice going. They can dredge up precedents and bylaws that you and I never heard of.'

Kyla clenched her hands together. The waiter approached their table, taking their plates and offering the menu for them to choose a sweet. 'I don't want any,' she said huskily, and Marc waved the menu away. 'Coffee?' he asked her. Kyla nodded and he ordered coffee for two, his voice so firm and crisp that she hated him for it.

When the man had moved away, he said, 'Nobody wants to do it that way, Kyla. But think about it, will you?'

'I'm thinking,' she said tensely, looking at him with resentment in her eyes. 'The little pigs won, didn't they?'

'They lost two houses in the process. How much could you afford to lose, Kyla?'

'You *are* threatening me!' she snapped, her green eyes suddenly brilliant with anger. She placed her hands flat on the table and made to get up, but his hand shot out and captured her wrist in a grasp that made her wince.

'Sorry,' he said, loosening his grip a little. 'Listen to me, Kyla. No one is threatening you. I'm trying to explain to you that we have no choice but to try the courts if we can't settle this thing any other way. We have too much money tied up in it not to try every way—every legal way—that's open to us. I have a responsibility to the shareholders, you know.'

'*Let me go!*' she muttered, so fiercely that she saw his eyes narrow at her tone before he removed his hand from her wrist and watched her snatch it away from the table on to her lap. 'Money!' she said scornfully. 'That's all you can think about—money and expansion!'

Cuttingly he said, 'Don't talk rubbish! It happens to be what's under discussion at the moment. What are *you* in business for? Don't tell me that's a non-profit charity you're running in that little shop of yours? Haven't you ever thought of expansion? It's certainly overcrowded as it is. What makes it a crime in our case? Success? Size? What makes the big moral difference between my business and yours?'

The questions came at her like bullets. Inwardly she flinched under their impact, but she maintained a calm front with some effort, keeping her face serene while her tightly clenched fingers were hidden in her lap.

The arrival of their coffee allowed her a breathing space, and when the waiter had moved away, she picked up her spoon, stirring sugar into the cup with an absorbed air. Marc took his black and unsweetened, and she couldn't help thinking that it was typical of his character.

'Well?' he asked peremptorily.

Kyla put both hands about her cup, not lifting it from the table. 'Of course I want to make a profit,' she admitted, 'but I don't have ambitions to join the millionaire class. All I need is a comfortable living from the shop. If I want to expand it's because I can give my customers a bigger variety of choice, and display my stock to better advantage.'

'I could say the same,' Marc told her briefly.

'But mine is a retail business,' said Kyla. 'It's more personal, more immediate. I have a particular type of clientele that I could lose if I move.'

'If you're talking about customer loyalty, surely they'll follow you if you change your address?'

'I don't mean just individual customers,' she argued. 'There's a certain *type* of customer——'

She broke off to sip at her coffee. Marc watched her, his eyes enigmatic.

'Go on,' he drawled. 'What's so special about your customers?'

'Well—the one thing that most of them have in common is that they don't have a lot of money to spend. That's the first thing in favour of my present location—the frontage is as attractive as I can make it, but it doesn't put off people on low incomes by looking too expensive for them. It doesn't intimidate people who are shy of big stores and exclusive boutiques. And my overheads are not high, so my prices are reasonable. I do have the odd tourists and a

few people who are quite well off coming hunting for a
bargain, but most of my customers are young married
couples or housewives with young children, or young people
looking for things for their flats or inexpensive gifts. A lot
of them don't have cars, so the fact that the buses are just
around the corner helps. And some of those who do have
cars are young mothers who don't want to walk too far
with their toddlers from the car park. And they like to
shop where they can leave the children to play in the park
and still keep an eye on them. The second-hand clothing
section does a lot of trade from them. They can outfit the
children and maybe find some nice little piece of pottery for
their home, and buy a couple of books all in the same place.'

'Do you make much from the second-hand stuff?' Marc
asked curiously.

'It doesn't return a vast profit, but it helps to bring
people into the shop, and they quite often buy other things
as well. Especially teenagers who come in looking for a
bargain dress or skirt—they often find their eye caught by
something from the new section as well.'

'How many of your customers try to get away with something—like the woman who tore off the price tag the day
I was there?'

Kyla put down her cup with a tiny crash, her eyes lighting with anger. 'She wasn't trying to get away with anything!' she snapped. 'If she had been, she would have
just stuffed the jersey into her bag and walked away with
it. Your trouble is, being born with a silver spoon in your
mouth, you don't know how the other half lives!'

His face went taut. 'I'm sure you're going to tell me,' he
said nastily.

Kyla looked down at the tablecloth. 'I shouldn't have
been rude,' she muttered.

'But you have been,' he returned, amused. 'In spite of
your careful upbringing.'

Stiffly she said, 'You don't know anything about my upbringing.'

'Oh, but it shows. I'm sure you were brought up to say please and thank you and never to speak to strangers.'

Her eyes dilated as she shot him a look that brought a quick frown to his. But she looked away immediately, lifting her cup to her face and concealing her expression behind it. She drained the cup and put it down, saying, 'Can we go now, please?'

His cup was empty, but he said, 'If you don't mind, I want another cup. What about you?'

He had already signalled the waiter, and although she refused, he asked for a second cup, then leaned his forearms on the table in front of him and said, 'You haven't finished telling me about this price business. Don't you think that removing the price from something is a form of cheating?'

Kyla took her own hands from the table and leaned back a little into her chair. 'It was nothing of the kind. She couldn't afford to pay the price on the ticket, but she wanted the jersey. And she was too proud to haggle over it by offering me a lower price, so she gave me the chance to alter it, that's all. If I'd stuck to the original price she wouldn't have bought it.'

He kept looking at her frowningly. 'So you lowered the price—how much?'

'About fifty per cent.'

'That's selling at a loss, isn't it?'

'Yes. But I'll make it up on something else. It wasn't much in terms of actual dollars and cents.'

His coffee came, but he seemed in no hurry to drink it. 'Do you often do that sort of thing?' he asked curiously.

'No, of course not. As you pointed out, I'm a businesswoman, I'm not running a charitable trust.'

He leaned back, a finger and thumb on his chin as he

stared thoughtfully at her. 'As a businesswoman,' he said, 'would you consider a business proposition?'

'That depends on what it is.'

'Don't look so wary. And try to forget for a minute the way you feel about me personally——'

Coldly, she said, 'I have no feelings about you personally, Mr Nathan.'

'Yes, you have. You dislike me intensely—it would be interesting to find out why, some time. It isn't exactly mutual, you know. Although several times I've been infuriated by you, you strike sparks off me in other ways, too.'

His eyes left her in no doubt what he meant. Her throat contracted, but she said steadily enough, 'I'm sure I'm not alone in that!'

Marc's eyebrows lifted a little, and he laughed softly. 'Let's just say you're not the first woman to do so,' he said.

'Let's just get back to business, shall we?' Kyla suggested.

He shrugged, still smiling, his eyes quizzical. He inclined his head a little ironically and said, 'Okay, we'll pursue the other matter some other time.' His eyes sharply challenged the rejection that he saw in her face, but he said, 'Supposing Nathans found you a site that had all the advantages of your present position—would you consider moving then?'

'I—suppose so,' she said. 'But it's impossible. There isn't any such site.'

'Trust me,' he said, his tone chiding.

Never! Kyla thought involuntarily. She looked away from his eyes because they were too frank and too keen, and said, 'Your coffee will be cold.'

He tasted it and put it down. 'Never mind. You wanted to go?'

He hadn't wanted it in the first place, she supposed. It

had only been an excuse to keep her there until he had got what he wanted.

She picked up the wrap that had fallen over the back of her chair, and when he made to help her with it she moved back from him, saying, 'It's all right, thanks.'

Outside she walked two feet away from him as they went to his car, and when he let her in settled herself close to the door and fastened the safety belt without fumbling this time, before he had got into the driver's seat.

He glanced at her and observed, 'You need a lot of space, don't you?' as he fastened his own belt.

'What do you mean?' she asked rather defensively as he turned the key and started the car.

'Do you know the theory that everyone has about them a so-called personal space, that we all get uneasy if anyone encroaches on it?' He glanced at her and she shook her head. 'Each person has their own space,' he went on. 'Some prefer more than others. An interesting sidelight is that in a prison experiment, it was found that violent offenders apparently need more personal space than most people.'

'You're very flattering,' she said.

He made an exasperated sound. 'And you take things too personally,' he retorted. 'I said it was an interesting sidelight, that's all. I didn't see you swinging your handbag at those three yobs yesterday.'

Kyla was silent, turning her head away as they travelled slowly between the flares of the street lights.

'I still don't understand,' he said, 'why you were so frightened.'

'You're not a woman,' she told him in brittle tones. 'You can't be expected to understand.'

'Perhaps not,' he conceded. 'But——'

'Do you mind if we talk about something else?' Kyla said sharply. She didn't want to have nightmares tonight.

Marc cast her a glance and shrugged. 'What would you like to talk about?'

'I have no preferences.'

Softly he said, 'Tell me about yourself, then.'

'I'm not interesting. I was brought up in a small, dull town. I left school and went to Auckland to find work. I worked a few years in a department store, then came North and started my own little business.'

'Are your parents still alive?' he asked.

Reluctantly, she said, 'Yes.'

'Do you ever go home?'

'I can't leave the shop.'

'You don't see much of your family, then.'

'We keep in touch by letter. They've been here on holiday once or twice.'

'Do you have brothers and sisters?'

'A sister. Do you?'

He glanced at her with a slight smile. 'I have a sister too, younger and married. She has three children. Would you like to meet them?'

'Why should I want to meet them?' she asked bluntly.

He shrugged. 'You have no family here. Do you have a lot of friends?'

'Enough,' Kyla said shortly. 'You've no need to feel sorry for me, Mr Nathan. I have an adequate social life, thank you.'

'I thought you were calling me Marc,' he murmured. 'Actually, it was a rather clumsy attempt to include you in *my* social life.'

Kyla couldn't resist a curious glance at the hard profile outlined by the street lights. She was sure he was seldom clumsy in his dealings with women. Harsh, maybe, on occasions, and more than likely rather cynical, but he was too obviously experienced to be clumsy.

He swung the car into her street and stopped outside

the flats. Kyla was framing words to thank him for the meal,
but he quickly cut the engine and released her safety belt
and his own in one swift movement. The wide band moving back over her shoulder pulled at her wrap and it slid
off.

Marc leaned over, one hand sliding along the seat back
behind her, the other going across in front of her to catch
at the wrap and drop it back again on her shoulder. But
instead of letting it go, he retained the fringed end of it in
his hand, his fingers playing with its softness as the fringing
fell over his wrist.

'It's silk, isn't it?' he asked.

'Yes.' Her voice was steady, but for the life of her she
couldn't say any more.

He lifted the end of the scarf and touched it to his cheek.
Kyla moved restlessly, pressing away from him.

His eyes gleamed in the darkness. 'I'm not touching you,'
he said. 'Am I in your space?'

'Yes, I think you are.'

'Do you mind?'

'Yes.'

'That's a pity. I rather like having you in *my* space.
Couldn't you bring yourself to invite me into yours?'

Kyla shook her head. He lowered his hand at the same
time, and the combined movements made the scarf slip
again, exposing the point of her shoulder.

Marc moved with infinite slowness as though afraid of
frightening her with a sudden lunge, and as she held her
breath, he bent his dark head and briefly, softly, touched his
lips to the bared shoulder. Kyla's teeth sank hard into her
lower lip. Then he pulled the scarf about her and leaned
back.

'Goodnight, Kyla,' he said.

She realised that he had opened the door for her while
he bestowed that fleeting, provocative caress on her shoul-

der. Wordlessly she got out of the car and walked without a backward glance along the path to her door. As she closed it, switching on the light automatically, she heard him start the engine and drive away.

She switched on the light in her bedroom, pulled the scarf off with a swift, agitated movement, and moved to the dressing table to take the pins out of her hair.

Her reflection stared back at her, the elegant dress still looking fresh and sophisticated, her hair smoothly combed back and without a strand out of place. But her lower lip looked fuller than usual, slightly swollen from the pressure of her teeth, giving her mouth an unexpectedly sensuous appearance, and her eyes looked misty and bewildered.

She shook her head, deliberately tightened her mouth, trying to dispel the disturbing image before her. Her hands went up to her hair, pulling it as she dealt with the pins that held it and threw them down with unwonted carelessness on the surface of the dressing table. She shook her loosened hair about her shoulders, then pushed it back with her hands, stepping away a little from the mirror. Suddenly arrested, she stared again at the image it presented to her, of a lovely young woman in an unconsciously provocative pose, her body curved gracefully, uplifted arms emphasising the line of her thigh, waist and breasts, and for a split second she had a picture in her mind of how a man might see her—as a desirable woman.

She dropped her arms and spun away from the mirror, screwing her hair into an elastic band, kicking off her shoes and tugging impatiently at her zipper. She stepped out of the dress and wriggled into her pyjamas, then spent ten minutes in the bathroom scrubbing roughly at her make-up with a soapy facecloth.

She lay in her bed, her hands clasped behind her head, staring up into the darkness. Her lip throbbed a little, and she ran her tongue over it and made a small, strange sound in the quiet room. She couldn't believe what had happened to her tonight.

You dislike me intensely, Marc Nathan had said, earlier. And she would have agreed instantly. Yesterday she had been grateful to him, but it hadn't made her like him any better. He was the kind of man she least admired—too self-assured, too concerned with money and success, too fond of getting his way, too impatient when he didn't, and much too sure of his effect on women.

When he made it clear he found her attractive she had been less flattered than frightened. The last thing she wanted was to get involved with a man like him. He made her feel nervous and vulnerable, and she hated that. All she wanted to do about Marc Nathan was keep as far away from him as possible. It was as simple as that.

But not quite so simple. Because against all expectation, all reason, all experience, the thing that had happened when he touched her skin with his lips could not be denied. It made no sense at all, but she had felt the shock of that light, swift kiss through her whole body—and, unbelievably but without any doubt at all, it had been a shock of pleasure.

CHAPTER THREE

THAT was how it began.

In the morning Kyla was still determined to have nothing further to do with the head of Nathans than absolutely necessary. From now on, she decided, the lawyers could sort out things between them, whatever happened. But the old-fashioned upbringing which he had guessed at nagged at her conscience, reminding her that in her haste to leave him last night she had neglected to thank him for the dinner.

She told herself that it was scarcely necessary to thank him for a business dinner, but the thought persisted that she had been discourteous. She tried to pretend that it wasn't important, but for some obscure reason the thought that Marc Nathan might share her own opinion of her manners was distinctly unwelcome.

At lunchtime she scribbled a note at her narrow desk, intending to take it over to the receptionist at the Nathan building and request that it be delivered to Mr Nathan. She thanked him for the dinner and apologised for forgetting to do so the night before, and was sitting with the end of the pen between her teeth, hesitating over whether she should add anything, when she heard the distinct tones of his voice asking Hazel where she was.

She sat very still, perhaps with a foolish, instinctive desire to pretend she was not there, but of course Hazel brought him over, pushing aside the curtain and saying, 'Mr Nathan would like to see you, Kyla.'

He stood in the opening, and Kyla hastily got to her feet, making the chair she had been sitting on rock dangerously.

Marc took a single long stride forward and steadied it. When he straightened, he still held the chairback, and she was trapped against the desk by the chair, his extended arm, and his body. He was much too close, and she shrank back a fraction, her hands clutching the edge of the desk for support.

For a long moment he stayed where he was, looking down at her with a slight frown in his eyes. Then his mouth curved a little in an ironic smile, and he moved back until his shoulder was touching the print curtain behind him.

Kyla breathed freely again, but he still looked much too big and overpowering for the tiny space.

'I was writing to you,' she told him.

'Writing? I'm only next door—and you have a phone, don't you?' His eyes found it among the neatly stacked account books and invoices on her desk.

'I didn't want to bother you,' Kyla said evasively. 'It was just a note to thank you for last night.'

'How very proper of you.' He paused. 'There is a very conventional and rather nice way for a lady to thank a man for a pleasant evening. Now that I'm here, you wouldn't like to——?'

He was smiling at her the way he had last night, his eyes fixed on her mouth as he made the teasing suggestion.

'No!' She kept her voice, aware of the thinness of the curtain.

His brows rose a little and he shrugged. 'Just a suggestion,' he said blandly. 'May I see the letter?'

'Why? It doesn't matter now that you're here. I just wanted to say thank you, and that I enjoyed the dinner.'

'I'd still like to see it.' He looked at the pad on the desk and moved forward to peer at it. Kyla moved too, one hand on the chairback and the other covering the open page.

Marc looked curiously at her face. 'I'll begin to think that you were writing me a love-letter, after all,' he said in a soft, amused voice.

Kyla moved sharply, lifting her hand from the note so that he could read it. He inclined his head and looked down at the neat, legible writing on the plain lined paper, and his hand went to the chairback, touching her fingers.

Kyla's hand was snatched away immediately, upsetting her balance, and she sat down rather quickly in the chair. Marc gave her another of those curious, penetrating glances, then read the words on the pad before them and said, 'You haven't finished it.'

'It only needs a signature,' she said.

He leaned back against the desk edge, looking down at her. 'Don't you think it's a little curt?'

'It says all that needs to be said.'

'How did you intend to sign it?' he asked with a hint of sarcasm. '*Yours faithfully?* Or do I rate a friendly *sincerely?* I couldn't hope for *Love from Kyla*, I suppose.'

'You surely don't expect that!' she retorted, trying to sound amused and slightly contemptuous. She picked up the pen from the desk in front of her and fiddled nervously with it. 'What did you want to see me about?' she asked him, forcing herself to meet his gaze calmly.

'I just wanted to see you.'

His eyes held a question—a question from a man to a woman, and Kyla inwardly recoiled, while her fingers tightened on the pen in her hands.

Marc's hand moved to cover them. Kyla jerked from the light clasp, but he managed to retain one of her hands in his, holding it firmly.

He asked quietly, 'What's the matter?'

Huskily she said, 'You're in my space.'

He might have been smiling, but she was avoiding his eyes, her fingers tense in his grasp. 'Couldn't you get used to it?' he asked her in the slow, coaxing drawl he had used last night.

Stubbornly, Kyla said, 'No.'

'Why not?' His voice was rather sharper. He meant to have an answer.

'You said it yourself last night, Mr Nathan, I dislike you intensely. I'm sorry, but you did ask.'

'I also said that I was interested in finding out why, didn't I? And that the feeling isn't mutual. As a matter of fact, I had the impression by the end of the evening, that you weren't disliking me quite so much as before.'

Kyla drawled, 'My good manners have been showing.'

Marc said nothing for a few seconds, then he released her hand and straightened up, shoving his hands into his pockets, and looked down at her still bent head. 'I suppose you're too well brought up to tell me straight out why you dislike me?' he said. 'It isn't only because I want to move you out of your shop, is it?'

'No, it isn't.'

'Then——?'

'It's just—the kind of man you are.'

After another pause, he asked, 'Aren't you going to give me a character analysis?'

Kyla shook her head. 'Does it matter?'

Deliberately, Marc said, 'No, I guess it doesn't. Good afternoon, Miss Vernon,' he added formally. 'You'll be hearing from our solicitors again.'

When he had gone she tore the page from the top of the pad and sat slowly tearing it into small pieces, staring at the wall with the pieces in her hands for quite a few minutes before she threw them into the wastebasket and went out to the shop to tell Hazel to take a lunch-break.

It was not until some time later that she wondered if his parting remark had been ominous. Had he meant that he was not going to bother, after all, with trying to find alternative premises for her shop—that she could expect to be taken to court by Nathans in an effort to move her? If that happened, she was not at all sure that she could afford to pay the legal costs that would be involved for her. She had a feeling they might be astronomical.

Hazel noticed her preoccupied air and asked, 'Is Mr Nathan putting the hard word on you, Kyla?'

'I don't think so,' Kyla answered. 'I wish I knew.'

It wasn't a very coherent answer, and Hazel looked surprised and puzzled. 'What do you mean?' she asked.

'Well, he said last night that he would try to find another site as good as this one for the shop. But I'm not sure if he hasn't gone back on it, now.'

'Last night?'

Of course, Hazel hadn't known about that. 'He took me out to dinner,' Kyla explained shortly. 'To talk about it.'

Hazel's face expressed surprise again, and unmistakably, speculation. 'Did he, indeed!' she murmured. 'Let me guess—he wanted to take it a bit further than dinner, you said nothing doing, and now you're afraid he's changed his mind. Does it matter? I mean, I thought you'd established that you can stay here if you want to. So he'd be cutting off his nose to spite his face, wouldn't he?'

'Not exactly. He thinks if they take me to court they could win, and I don't think he's bluffing. And it wasn't quite what you think, either. He didn't make a pass at me —really.'

'So what did you do to put his back up? He didn't look too chipper when he went out of here at lunchtime.' Kyla shrugged and said nothing. 'Sorry,' Hazel said resignedly. It's none of my business, of course.'

She made to move away, and Kyla reached out to touch her arm in contrition. 'I'm sorry, Hazel,' she said, 'I didn't mean to snub you. It's just a bit difficult to explain, that's all. I know you're not prying, you're genuinely interested and I'm grateful, really I am.'

Hazel gave her a wry smile. 'Want to tell Auntie about it?' she asked. 'You're a private sort of person, Kyla, and I know you like to handle your own problems your own way. But there are times when another head helps. Or a shoulder to cry on. You know you're welcome to use mine. But I don't want to push in——'

'You're not pushing in at all. I'll remember the offer if I need it.'

Hazel gave her hand a pat and moved back to her task of counting change out of the till.

'Hazel?'

'Yes?' The older woman looked up immediately.

'Am I—cold and unfriendly?'

'Good heavens, did I make you think that?'

'No, someone else said it.'

'Well, don't you take any notice,' Hazel advised her indignantly. 'As I said, you're a private kind of person, independent, maybe reserved. You don't parade your every emotion, but you're not unfriendly, and I've never thought you were. I wouldn't have taken this job if I had. I suppose it was a man who told you that,' she added shrewdly. 'Don't you listen to him, my dear. It's the oldest trick in the book.'

'Actually,' said Kyla a little guiltily, remembering Marc's denial of her interpretation of his remark, he didn't say those actual words. He just seemed to be implying something of the sort.'

Hazel said, 'Hmm,' and gave her a thoughtful look, but a bunch of teenagers breezed into the shop at that moment, and from then on they were kept busy for the rest of the day.

Chris dashed in near closing time and asked if she wanted a lift home, his eyes full of curiosity which a casual manner could not quite hide. Kyla didn't feel she needed to explain anything to him. She told him she was picking up her own car after the shop was closed, and thanked him for the offer.

His fingers toying with a brown pottery salt pig on the counter, he shuffled his feet a little and asked her, 'Care to go to a film on Saturday night?'

'I don't think so, thanks,' she told him.

'Got another date?' he enquired, picking up the salt pig with a studiously casual air.

'No.'

He looked up then, studying her face. 'Are you punishing me for something, Kyla?'

At a loss, she said, 'No, of course not! I just don't feel much like going out this week, that's all.'

Chris put down the piece of pottery very carefully exactly where he had got it from. 'Some other time, then?' he said, watching her keenly.

There was a momentary hesitation before Kyla said, 'Yes—of course.'

It was rather dismaying to realise that she could summon no desire to go out with Chris ever again. After all, he had been a good friend to her and she was not so well off for escorts that she could afford cavalier treatment of one who was willing to squire her about without expecting too much in the way of the kind of conventional 'thanks' that Marc had spoken of.

When she had closed the door and locked it behind Chris, a few minutes early, she found her thoughts returning again to the interview with Marc. Altogether it had not been very satisfactory. Originally she had agreed to give Nathans a final answer to their offer on Friday, which was tomorrow.

Did that offer still stand? She was not sure.

It was an unsatisfactory state of affairs, and after worrying over the various questions in her mind all night, she decided she would have to find out where she stood. She began by phoning Mr King as soon as she arrived at the shop, asking him if the offer made to her a few days ago was still open.

'Why, certainly, as far as I know,' he said. 'Why do you ask?'

'Mr Nathan said something that made me wonder if it was,' she told him.

'Well,' said the lawyer cautiously, 'it was a verbal offer only, Miss Vernon.' She wondered if he was relieved to think that his client might have had second thoughts. She was quite sure he had thought the offer extravagant. 'I would say you should talk to Mr Nathan again,' Mr King added.

Frustrated, Kyla thanked him and put down the receiver.

She stared for a while at the telephone book on her desk, then picked it up and found Nathan's number. The voice that answered when she dialled it was efficient, friendly and very feminine. Mr Nathan was in conference, but she could take a message and she was sure he would ring Miss Vernon back as soon as possible.

The phone rang just as Hazel arrived at ten. The same feminine voice told her that Mr Nathan had received her message, and apologised for not phoning her back in person. He would be free at ten-thirty and would like to know if she could call at his office at about that time.

'Couldn't he just phone me at that time?' asked Kyla, trying to sound as coolly polite as the secretary.

But the voice became doubtful. She thought Mr Nathan was rather anxious to see Miss Vernon in person; if the time didn't suit she would consult his appointment book and try to arrange another. What time would suit better?

If she had to leave the shop, ten-thirty was as good a time as any, Kyla conceded grudgingly. The voice was satisfied. Mr Nathan would be expecting her.

She arrived on time and was rather surprised to be shown straight into his office. He wasn't there, but the secretary said he would be with her in a few moments. Kyla sat down, expecting to wait much longer and working herself into a genteel rage at his dragging her away from the shop to kick her heels in this den of luxury he called an office.

But he must have come as soon as he was told she had arrived. He strode in less than half a minute later, with a faint grin on his face, saying, 'How very punctual you are, Kyla. I hope I haven't kept you waiting.'

'Hardly at all,' she admitted, but contriving to make it sound as though she had been here for ages and was merely being polite in denying it. He knew, of course, that she had only just arrived, but the grin widened just a trifle, then his mouth took on a slight down-curve and he propped himself against his desk instead of going around it to sit in the chair at the other side, and surveyed her.

'I have to admit,' he said, 'that I didn't expect you to arrive on time.'

She realised that he had thought she would probably keep him waiting for her deliberately, in retaliation for being summoned to his office instead of his phoning her as she had requested. That was why he had not been here when she arrived.

Her voice dulcet, she said, 'I don't play those sort of games, Mr Nathan. They must waste a lot of time.'

His eyes glinted. 'You must enlighten me some time as to the kind of games you *do* play, Kyla.'

Kyla didn't blush, and she hoped he was disappointed.

He folded his arms, and looked down at her. 'Well?' he drawled lazily. 'I gathered you wanted to see me.'

'I only wanted to speak to you.'

There was a discreet tap at the door, and the secretary came in with two cups of tea on a tray, which she placed on the desk. Marc said, 'Thank you, Sandra,' and the girl withdrew.

Kyla didn't want to sit there drinking tea with him, but when he passed her a cup and stood holding the sugar bowl for her, she could hardly refuse without downright rudeness. She hoped he would take his to the other side of his desk, but he didn't. He put his cup down beside him as he resumed his former stance.

She stirred sugar into her tea and put the spoon carefully on the saucer.

'I wanted to know,' she said, 'if your offer still stands.'

'Of course it does.'

'And—your other suggestion? That you might find an alternative site for me?'

'What about it?'

'Does that still stand, too?'

'You mean, does one cancel out the other? I wasn't looking at it that way. The answer is no. I'll stand by them both.'

She looked up at him and said quietly, 'Thank you. I thought——'

She hesitated, deciding it was better not to tell him what she had been thinking, but he said, 'What did you think?'

Kyla took a couple of sips from her cup. 'I was a bit confused after you left yesterday,' she admitted. 'You said I'd be hearing from your solicitors and I thought— you might have had second thoughts.'

Marc had not yet picked up his own tea. He looked down at it, touched the cup with his fingers and then withdrew them, looking at her with hard eyes. 'You mean you thought I might take a petty revenge because you don't like me, and you said so? Your view of my character is— interesting.'

'You mean it's mistaken, don't you? I'm sorry, but I wasn't sure what you meant, and I don't know enough about you to judge your character.'

'That's new, at any rate. I thought it was just what you *had* done. You said something about disliking the kind of man I am.'

'I didn't intend you to take it personally.' Unhappily, she stared down at the remainder of her tea.

'I find it a little difficult to take it any other way,' said Marc, picking up his own cup and downing the liquid in seconds. 'More tea?' he asked politely.

'No, thanks.' Kyla swallowed what was left in her cup and he stood up and moved over to take it from her. But he didn't move away. He stayed by her chair staring thoughtfully down at her while she tried to pretend she was unaware of his eyes on her. Breaking the suddenly tense silence, she said, 'I'll accept your offer, on condition that you find suitable premises for me elsewhere—that *I* agree are suitable.'

She had almost said she would accept a lower offer in those circumstances, but she really didn't think a suitable alternative was available, and for some reason the fact that he thought she was an astute businesswoman helped her to build some kind of barrier between them which she needed. Let him think she was holding out for the highest price she could get. The chances were he would never have to pay it, and in the meantime the shop would be safe. She had agreed to his terms, and couldn't be threatened with legal proceedings now.

He moved so that he stood in front of her, subjecting her to a long, thoughtful look. 'Okay,' he said slowly, 'shall we draw up an agreement to that effect?'

'Must we?'

He went on looking at her a few seconds longer before he spoke again. 'No, I'll take your word. Just one thing, though. If you're just stalling us off——'

Her lashes quickly lifted and fell again, but he must have seen something in her eyes before she veiled them.

'Aha!' he said softly. He suddenly bent forward, putting his hands on the arms of the leather chair in which she sat, so that she pressed back, staring defiantly into his dark, hard eyes. 'Listen, lady,' he said, 'if I find a place for you that has all those desirable features you mentioned to me over dinner the other night, you'd better have ninety-nine damn good reasons before you turn it down as not suitable!'

'I will have! *Will you please get away from me?*'

She spoke between clenched teeth, hiding fear with anger. Marc straightened after a moment, but didn't move away.

'It really bothers you, doesn't it?' he drawled.

'I don't like standover tactics. And as a matter of fact it hadn't crossed my mind to stall off in that way. If you really come up with something as good as what I have, I'll take it. But I don't think you can.'

'Give me time.' He turned to stack their cups on the tray, and Kyla took the chance to stand up and move a little away from the chair, and from him. He glanced at her and then turned fully to face her. 'I'll let you know when I find something.'

She said thank you, and turned to leave the room. His step was silent on the carpet, but he reached the door before she did, pausing with his hand on the knob so that she stopped a bare few inches from him. She saw the brief light of amused speculation in his eyes before he pulled it open and let her walk through. He knew very well that he made her uneasy whenever he was close to her, she realised. He knew it, and it amused him to manoeuvre her into these situations so that he could watch her reaction. At least, this time, she had refrained from physically shrinking from him. If she showed no reaction no doubt he would tire of his game. Not that she intended to give him a chance to play with her like that again!

It was weeks before she spoke to him again. She avoided him in the car park and thought with a certain satisfaction that he must be having trouble trying to track down suitable premises for her. She wondered how long it would be before he admitted defeat.

She had kept her promise to Chris to go out with him another time, but she thought he knew that she intended to gradually ease out of her relationship, such as it was, with him. A certain waspishness had entered into some of his remarks to her, and she gathered that he was not too happy at being kept at arms' length when she said goodnight to him after an evening out. They had nearly quarrelled, and only her own remorse when he apologised had stopped her breaking off with him there and then. She felt that she had made use of him and treated him badly, but she could no longer enjoy his company.

She answered the telephone at the shop one day and heard a curt male voice say, 'Kyla?'

It was extraordinary, she thought, that she knew immediately who it was. Every nerve tightened as she took a firmer grip on the receiver and said, 'Yes?'

Her voice sounded distant and cool, and he said, 'It's Marc. Are you free after work this evening?'

'I don't think——' she began cautiously, but he interrupted.

'This is business,' he told her, his tone decidedly dry.

Her heart unaccountably seemed to sink, but she said, 'I didn't think otherwise. What is it you want?'

There was a rather eloquent silence, and she had the feeling he was turning over in his mind which of several disconcerting retorts he might make. But when he spoke he only said, 'I think I've found something to suit you. Can you look it over with me this evening? I have a key.'

It was Kyla's turn to be silent, caught in an odd feeling of panic. Did he have to show it to her, himself? But she couldn't get out of it. If she pleaded pressure of work or some other arrangements, Marc would fix another time, so it might just as well be now. She said, 'I close the shop at five. Can you give me half an hour after that?'

If he wondered what for, he didn't ask. 'Okay,' he said. 'Five-thirty.'

In case he thought she was planning to prink for him, she said hastily, 'I have some pricing to do.'

'I'll see you at the shop, then.' He paused. 'Will you let me in?'

'Of course,' she said, refusing to see any other meaning in that than the surface one, but aware that the timbre of his voice had changed to a teasing, low note.

'Thank you,' he said quickly, and put down the phone.

He was prompt, and she was ready when he arrived, opening the door with her bag in her hand so that she had no need to invite him in. If Marc saw any significance in that, it didn't show in his face. His gaze slipped over her neat, crisp blouse and skirt, but his expression was neutral, perhaps even carefully so.

'Where are we going?' she asked him.

'Not far. This way.'

He put a hand lightly on her arm and walked her to the park and across it, not speaking again until they gained the pavement on the other side. Then he only said, 'Over here,' as his grip became slightly firmer on her arm to steer her to their left.

They walked a little way along the pavement and then entered a small arcade. Marc stopped at one of the doors that opened on to it and took out a key from his pocket. Kyla looked at the small display windows on either side of the door, filled with cosmetics, suntan preparations and hair-drayers, and at the lettering over the door. She sometimes bought things for herself at this tucked-away chemist's shop. The owner was quite a young man, and she couldn't imagine why he might want to sell out.

Marc had the door open, and was waiting for her to go in. She stepped past him, looking about a little doubtfully. The shop was newer than her own, and considerably more roomy. It was L-shaped, and had two cash counters among the display stands. Perhaps following her train of thought as she walked into the right-angle, Marc said, 'If you put a counter in that corner, you could have a good view of the whole shop.'

Kyla said nothing, still looking about, assessing the height of the walls, the amount of fixed shelving, the lighting and the windows. He watched her for a few minutes, and then walked over to the other end and turned a key in a narrow door tucked away in the corner, where she had scarcely noticed it. Opening it, he said, 'Come here.'

When she obeyed, he took her hand and moved ahead of her to the outside, saying, 'Mind the step.'

They stood in a deserted yard that had once been surfaced with concrete, now cracked and broken. In one corner there was an ugly shed piled high with boxes and cartons, and overshadowed, unexpectedly, by a mature tree that had forced the concrete apart about its roots. Untidy grass pushed itself up in desperate little patches here and there. On two sides the yard was bounded by corrugated iron fencing, and at the far end was a sagging, rusty wire fence.

Freeing her hand from Marc's hold, Kyla walked over to the tree. 'However did it get here?' she asked.

'Self-sown, I should think,' he said, standing where she had left him. 'No one bothered to get rid of it.'

'I should think not! Why should they?'

'It hasn't done the concrete much good.'

'The *concrete* isn't beautiful,' Kyla retorted. 'The tree is the only thing worth looking at round here.'

'You could get rid of the concrete altogether, if you like. Fence the yard off properly with stained boards, and plant it in grass. If you knocked out a piece of wall and put in a big window, your customers could leave their offspring safely within sight while they're in the shop.'

Kyla looked at the tree again. It had grown oddly shaped, but there was an ideal branch for a swing, and room, she fancied, for a small tree hut not too far from the ground. She could imagine, instead of the shed, a sandpit stocked with sturdy toy cars and construction vehicles. The idea definitely had possibilities.

She put up her hand and touched the tree, thoughtfully fingering a broad, rather dusty leaf. Marc joined her, standing a few feet away and watching her. 'Do you know what it is?' he asked.

Kyla looked up. 'The tree? Some kind of beech, I think.'

'You like trees. Do you know much about them?'

Kyla shook her head and turned to go back into the shop. Marc locked the door behind them and said, 'Come upstairs.'

'Upstairs?'

He smiled and stepped behind one of the counters, pulling aside a curtain. She had expected that it hid a small office like her own, but instead he had revealed a narrow stairway, and motioned her to climb up ahead of him. Perhaps because she was terribly conscious of him just behind her, she went up very quickly and arrived at the top slightly breathless.

There was a landing with a small, neat bathroom off it, and two rooms that were empty except for an odd broken chair, some disused display stands and a few boxes of still-packed stock for the chemist's shop. In an alcove that was

facing the yard at the rear, a small sink bench was let into
a bank of cupboards and a zip water heater hung over it. A
two-ring stove completed the kitchen area. Evidently the
place had been designed as a flat for living in over the shop.

'Surprised?' queried Marc.

'Yes. I had no idea.'

Casually he asked, 'Think there's enough room for you?'

'More than enough. You know that.'

'Don't complain on that score. Parkinson's law says that
whatever space you have, you'll fill it.'

'And Nathan's law says I'd better be grateful,' she murmured, turning away from him to move over to the kitchen
wall, leaning over the sink to peep into the yard below.
'Where's the nearest bus stop?' she asked, sure that he had
gone into that question.

He didn't disappoint her. He came over to stand beside
her, pointing out of the window beyond the corner of the
yard. 'See that gap between the two buildings at the rear?
It's a walkway to the main street, and continues down the
side of this building. The buses stop just where it comes
out. The car park is a little further away from here than
from your present premises, but there are two-hour meters
just along the street. And the park is still handy.'

Kyla turned away from the window, almost brushing
him. He didn't move, and she suppressed a flicker of
irritated awareness, her eyes flashing briefly at the faint
amusement in his. It pleased him to tease her, but she was
not going to rise to his baiting.

When she moved towards the stairs, he said, 'I'll go first.
They're steep.'

Kyla shrugged and stepped aside. The light was fading
a little and the stairs were dim. He waited for her at the
bottom, turning to face her. She came down carefully, holding the plain wooden railing, but even so she stumbled
somehow on the last step.

Marc stepped forward and she felt his fingers hard and warm on her arms, his breath against her temple. She breathed in sharply and he slowly released her. But he still blocked her way, standing before the curtain that screened the stairs, his face shadowed. 'Will it do?' he asked her.

She wished he had not decided to conduct this discussion here. 'It might,' she said cautiously. 'I'd like to think about it. And I must find out if I can afford it.'

'You can—I've been into that. You might even make an extra income if you let the top floor as a flat—or would you want to live in it yourself?'

'No!' Kyla said positively.

'It might not be so bad for one person, if it was fixed up. You do live alone, don't you?'

'Yes, but with neighbours on either side of me.'

'You'd be nervous here?'

'Maybe—a bit.'

She had the feeling he was trying to read her expression, and was suddenly glad of the poor light where they stood.

Marc observed, 'You're a bundle of contradictions.'

'Isn't everyone? *You* certainly are.'

He gave a soft laugh. 'That makes it mutual, then.'

He still hadn't moved, but she had a sudden feeling that he was crowding her. The little space at the foot of the stairs acquired a disturbingly intimate atmosphere, and as she glanced up into his eyes she knew distinctly that the look he was giving her was meant to make her aware of herself—and of him. His mouth had a sensual curve to it, and his eyes lazily touched her mouth, slipped to her taut throat as she lifted her chin to stare at him coldly, and rested for a few searing moments on the shadowed skin above the top button of her open-necked blouse.

She wouldn't give him the satisfaction of knowing that her heart was pounding uncomfortably, and her breathing felt constricted. She couldn't help, though, the sudden intake of breath that brought his eyes lower as the front of her blouse tautened momentarily over the rise and fall of her breasts.

Her instinct was to push by him and out of the claustrophobic little space into the shop, but if she did, he would know he had succeeded in affecting her in some way. In brittle tones she said quickly, 'I didn't know Mr Harding was planning to move. How did you find out?'

'He wasn't planning a move, until I suggested it to him.'

'I see.' In a desperate effort to regain her poise, she resorted to sarcasm. 'And once you suggested it, of course he was delighted to fall in with whatever you wanted!'

'As it happens, I was able to offer him something *he* wanted.'

Kyla leaned back a little on the balustrade behind her and folded her arms. It removed her a little from Marc's uncomfortable nearness, and gave an illusion of nonchalance.

She injected a note of deliberate mockery into her voice and said, 'Do tell me more.'

His brief hesitation might have eant he was disconcerted, but he didn't show it. 'It's quite simple. I had an agent looking for something for you. He drew a blank, but he did tell me there was a property coming on the market further up the main street, close to a doctor's rooms. There are no doctors near here, and it occurred to me that a chemist might prefer to be in a busy area, and that he might pick up a lot of business right next door to a doctor. So I put it to him, offered a good price for this, and found him very interested. If you like this place, I'll give you a good lease on it.'

'It will have to be watertight!' she said grimly.

'I'm sure you'll see to that.'

Well, she would, too. Her lawyer would be asked to go over it with a fine toothcomb, she decided. 'You've got it all worked out like a game of chess, haven't you?' she commented. 'Everybody moved out of the way to allow you to make *your* move.'

'Why does that sound a criticism, I wonder?'

'Criticism? Good heavens, I'm lost in admiration! It must be lovely for you to be able to shift all of us little pawns about the way you do. And it's all done with kindness, too. Everyone benefits, don't they? We're all much better off than before.'

'As a matter of fact, yes ...' The very flatness of his tone told her that she had angered him. She wondered at her own temerity, her reckless desire to hit out at him. It was true he had hurt no one, getting what he wanted, but she could not shake off the deep certainty that if he was seriously opposed the velvet would be removed with a vengeance. The man was unstoppable!

She moved away from the balustrade, hoping he would take the hint, and said, 'Well, I'll think over your generous offer, Mr Nathan.' Recalling his own tactic with the louts he had rescued her from, she took a determined step forward, making to pass him.

She might have known it wouldn't work. He didn't move out of the way, but instead gripped her by the arms and then pulled her into the hard circle of his. Her angry protest was smothered by his mouth on hers, kissing her with insulting expertise and an edge of anger. Her lack of response seemed not to affect him at all, and he simply ignored the taut resistance of her body as his arms moulded her closer to his. Dismayed, she discovered that the thing that had happened before was happening again. Her panic was shot through with sudden pleasure, and the realisation made her shiver with an odd compound of emotions.

Marc lifted his head, although his arms retained their imprisonment of her. 'Something else for you to think about, Kyla,' he said softly before he released her and gave her a slight push into the relative brightness of the shop.

CHAPTER FOUR

KYLA knew she didn't have a single good reason to turn down Mr Harding's shop. Marc had an option on it until the following week, he had told her before they parted the night he had shown her over it. The implication, she knew, was that she must make up her mind before then. She would certainly have been hard up for ninety-nine good reasons not to say yes.

She waited until the very last day before she phoned him with her acceptance, and in all that time he hadn't contacted her. For some reason that made her angry; she had expected him to be impatient for her verdict and to try to hurry her decision if possible.

On the phone he was crisp and businesslike, and she felt unaccountably let down when she put down the receiver. She called her lawyer to tell him of her decision, and that Mr King would be contacting him about the lease. Then she told Hazel, who was surprised and delighted. 'You should celebrate,' said Hazel. 'Are you seeing Chris tomorrow night?'

Kyla shook her head, with a troubled little smile. She hadn't seen Chris for some days, and supposed he had taken the hint and would not be asking her out again.

Hazel cast her a shrewd look and said, 'Well, come to our place, and we'll have a bottle of something and I'll cook something special. You haven't been round for ages. How about schnitzel? I can buy some veal on the way home.'

'I'd like that,' said Kyla. 'But you don't need to cook anything special.'

'Rot, I'll enjoy it. My talents are wasted on my family.

If it's hot and filling, that's all they care about. They'd like to see you again, though. Young Terry has quite a crush on you!'

'That's starting young, isn't it?' Kyla asked, amused. 'I thought boys of twelve were still at an age to despise all females.'

'Kids grow up faster these days, I'm afraid. Anyway, I'm not worried about him admiring you from afar. In a few years, when he shows interest in girls of his own age, we might have problems. I know I'm only his doting old mum, but he's not a bad-looking lad, is he?'

'It runs in the family,' Kyla smiled. 'Terry's very good-looking, and he has a load of charm and personality, as well——'

She turned as someone entered the shop, and found herself looking into Marc Nathan's eyes. He came straight to the corner where they stood, moved his eyes for a fraction of a second to give Hazel a nod of recognition, and said, 'I thought we should celebrate our deal, Kyla. Are you free tomorrow evening?'

Very politely, she said, 'I'm sorry, I've made other arrangements.'

But Hazel interposed swiftly, 'Oh, that's all right, Kyla. You can come to dinner another time. How about Sunday evening? Tracy has the day off from the hospital, then—and she'd like to see you. You go out with Mr Nathan to-morrow night—go on!'

Marc said, 'Thank you, Mrs Wright. What time would you like me to pick you up, Kyla?'

Trying not to show her annoyance and dismay, she said, 'I have a car. There's no need for you to——'

'When I take a lady out, I call for her,' he interrupted. 'One of the things my mother taught me. So just tell me what time.'

Hazel was trying to look as though she wasn't listening,

but Kyla saw the look of satisfaction on her face. Hazel evidently approved of Marc Nathan and his mother's training!

Marc was waiting for her reply. Reluctantly, she said, 'I'll leave that to you. What sort of celebration did you have in mind?'

'A quiet dinner, maybe a little dancing——'

'I don't dance.'

He raised his eyebrows a little, and Hazel stared in surprise. Marc said quietly, 'Just dinner, then. With a show, or without?'

'Just as you like,' she shrugged. 'I'm not fussy.'

He looked at her with an odd expression for a moment and said, 'I'll pick you up at seven, then, if that suits you.'

'All right.' Let him go out of his way, then, if he insisted.

He left immediately, apparently satisfied. Hazel looked so pleased it was all Kyla could do to refrain from telling her, that she might have kept her mouth shut and allowed Kyla to avoid an evening spent with Marc Nathan.

But none of it was Hazel's fault; she had acted with the best of motives. Kyla swallowed her frustration and resigned herself.

After six on Saturday, she had a shower and riffled through her wardrobe for something cool to wear. The humidity was still high. She tried to tell herself that the stifling heat was responsible for the strange thickness in her throat and the little ripples of apprehension that now and then chased each other from throat to stomach and back again. But it had been hot all day, and those sensations had started when had she looked up yesterday in the shop and seen Marc coming towards her. She remembered exactly the way he had looked, and how her body had suddenly remembered, with embarrassing exactness, the strange emotions his had roused in it when he kissed her.

She hadn't thought she could ever feel like that about a man. In a way she felt an odd, detached relief that it was possible, after all, that her body was capable of reacting in that way, because the men she had been fond of in the past had never been able to touch any core of pleasure or passion. But that it should be *this* man appalled her. Again and again she had told herself she disliked everything about him—his power, his ruthless charm, his confidence in his ability in business and with people. Even physically he was not her type. She had never admired big, handsome, determined-looking men, conscious of their masculinity and exploiting it to the full. And she despised those who flaunted their success with women. Admittedly he had not boasted to her, but Chris had certainly implied that he was the type, and it fitted. He must be fairly well into his thirties, and hadn't married. But he was no novice at making love.

Impatiently Kyla shook back her loosened hair, pulling off its hanger a silky, cool print dress in jewel shades of blue and green. The top was a halter-style, the front demure enough, with a scalloped collar, the back bare to just above her waist. It would make the heat bearable.

She was ready when he arrived, her black sandals on her feet, her hair pinned up again in its impeccable roll. Marc glanced at it and asked, 'Don't you ever wear your hair down?' then stepped back to let her precede him down the path.

'It's cooler like this,' she answered as he opened the door of his car for her. He was dressed casually for the heat, too, in a shirt only half buttoned up, that she thought was natural silk, and fawn, close-fitting slacks. She felt a stirring of reluctant attraction as he seated himself beside her and started the car.

He had driven back through the business area and they were passing the boat harbour with its multitude of pleasure craft, and the ill-fated replica of the *Bounty*, built for a film that had never been made, when she asked him where they were going.

'My place,' he said briefly.

She turned her head sharply to stare at him. 'You mean your house?'

'My home. Mrs Wright invited you to her place for dinner—I thought I would invite you to mine.'

'But that's different!'

He seemed amused. 'Is it? Why, because I'm a man and might have designs on your virtue? I haven't you know—not tonight, at any rate.'

Kyla didn't know if he lived alone. He had never said if his mother was still alive. 'Am I expected?' she asked, finally.

'Yes,' he said, and didn't volunteer any more information. Kyla tried hard to relax her taut nerves as the road took them along the river bank, with the lights of the houses on the other side glowing on one by one in the softly gathering dusk. Eventually they turned into a gateway between spreading magnolias and rhododendrons, and swept up a curving gravelled drive to the front of an old and gracious villa with a pillared veranda and gables on the roof.

'The ancestral home, such as it is,' Marc told her, and got out to open her door. The front door was ajar, and he pushed it open and led her into a wide old-fashioned passageway with doors opening off either side. He guided her through the first of these, into a gracious sitting room furnished in a mixture of colonial and modern furniture, with an archway leading to an equally lovely dining room. 'Some of this stuff has been here since my grandfather's time,' he told her. 'Make yourself comfortable, and I'll go and let Mrs Bridgeway know that we've arrived.'

When he came back Kyla was standing in front of a

carved rimu cabinet, admiring the collection of Victoriana
it held. When she turned he said, 'Will you have a drink
before we start? Dinner will be ready in fifteen minutes.'

She hesitated, then asked for a small medium sherry. She
sat down in one of the large, comfortable modern armchairs
facing the bow window that looked out on a lawn studded
with trees, and when he brought her drink over and took
a chair close to hers, she said, 'Who is Mrs Bridgeway?'

'My housekeeper?'

'Housekeeper? I thought they went out with the Ark!'

'They're a rare breed these days, but I've been lucky.'

He would be, she thought. He probably paid the woman
a phenomenal sum in wages. 'I expect she's a treasure,' she
said.

'Definitely. And in case you're wondering, she doesn't
live in servants' quarters behind the kitchen or in the
attic. She comes in for a few hours a day, and usually leaves
a meal prepared for me to cook myself. But on special
occasions she's willing to stay on and make a meal if I have
a guest.'

Kyla wondered how often the guest was a woman.
Watching her, Marc said in a quietly amused tone, 'Usually
they're business contacts. This is a pleasant change.'

'I am a business contact,' she reminded him succinctly.

'I guess,' he said. 'You're also a very lovely lady. As I
said, it's a change.'

She sipped at her sherry, aware of his eyes on her, and
stared out of the window. But the light was almost gone,
and after a few moments Marc rose to his feet, pulling together the rose velvet curtains to cover the glass, then
standing in front of them, his drink in his hand, while he
smiled down teasingly at her shuttered face. 'What's the
matter?' he said, softly taunting. 'Don't you like compliments?'

'Not specially. They're usually insincere.'

'That's a cynical view for a girl like you to take!'

'You don't know what sort of girl I am.'

'Well, it's something I aim to find out.'

Her eyes went down to her barely touched sherry, her fingers tightening on the glass. She heard Marc put his glass down on the table near the window, and looked up in sudden alarm as he moved closer to her. He stood where he was, a frown in his eyes. 'Still disliking me?' he asked. 'Wouldn't you like to find out what sort of man I really am?'

Crisp and cold as a frosty morning, she said, 'I can't think of any reason why I should.'

He shoved his hands into his pockets, and his voice was suddenly harsh. 'Stop fencing, Kyla. You know very well why. You fought me all the way when I kissed you, but I felt you quivering with delight all the same.'

Kyla's flesh went goose-pimpled with fright. 'That,' she said steadily, 'was a shudder of revulsion.'

He made a quick movement, and she looked up to see his face darken with anger. In a savage undertone he muttered, 'Like hell it was!' And then the door at the other side of the dining room through the archway opened, and a woman's voice said, 'It's ready now, Mr Nathan, if you'd like to bring your visitor to the table.'

He stayed looking down at Kyla for a moment or two before he wrenched his gaze away and said, 'Thank you, Mrs Bridgeway.'

She disappeared, and he said to Kyla, 'Finish your sherry.'

'I've had enough, thanks,' she said, and stood up, holding the glass out to him.

His mouth was tight and he looked a trifle pale; she wondered if temper did that to him. But he took her glass and placed it beside his, then courteously waved her before him to the table, beautifully set for two, with a centrepiece of creamy magnolias in a low crystal bowl.

Mrs Bridgeway returned with two bowls of chilled cucumber soup, and Marc introduced her to Kyla. She whisked out again, and the soup, accompanied by crisply warmed bread rolls, was eaten in a tense silence. Mrs Bridgeway returned with plates of crumbed fish fillets, new potatoes tossed in parsley and butter, fresh peas and finely cut salad. A bottle of white wine was placed on the table before Marc's place, and he poured some for both of them. Kyla sipped it cautiously and found it delicious and cool.

Her voice husky with effort, she said, 'Mrs Bridgeway is a wonderful cook. Does she have a family of her own?'

Marc was sipping at his wine, regarding her rather sardonically over the rim. He put the glass down carefully on the white table cloth before he answered. 'Yes, she does. A husband and four strapping sons.'

'She must be very busy.'

'I think she has them well trained. She's very efficient.'

'Is your own mother alive?' she asked.

'She died over ten years ago.'

'I'm sorry. That must have been a blow.'

'Of course. But life goes on. It hit my father hardest.'

'This is a big house for one person, isn't it?' she asked as she cut into her fish.

'Yes, but I like the place. It's peaceful to come home to. And my sister brings her tribe sometimes at the weekend and lets them run wild. They enjoy it.'

'How much ground is there?'

'A couple of acres.'

Kyla took a sip of the delicious wine. 'I suppose you have a gardener as well as a housekeeper,' she said with a hint of dryness.

'A contractor mows the lawns once a week,' he said. 'The rest I can manage. It's mostly in trees and shrubs, anyway, not hard to keep tidy.'

'Do you like gardening?' Kyla asked curiously.

'I like getting outside, and there's a certain satisfaction in slashing weeds and trimming trees. I'm not patient enough for the fiddly stuff, though. Planting seeds and lifting bulbs I prefer to leave to the enthusiasts. I like horses, dogs and children, too. You see, it's not so painful, is it?'

'What?' asked Kyla, disconcerted.

'Finding out what sort of man I am. What about you? I'd guess you're a cat person—are you?'

'I had a cat when I was a child,' she admitted.

He waited, watching her, and when she didn't elaborate he said gently, 'Did it have a name?'

'Smokey. Not exactly original.'

'I take it the cat was grey.'

'What else?' Kyla said lightly.

'What sort of childhood did you have, Kyla?'

'It was grey,' she said flippantly. 'Not marvellous, not dismal, not original. And not interesting. How was yours?'

'Marvellous in some spots and dismal in others, I guess. Maybe we have a different outlook on life.'

'Maybe.'

'Yours seems rather negative,' he suggested.

Kyla looked up from her plate. 'And yours is positive—oh, yes, definitely.'

He leaned over and topped up her wine glass. Seeing her doubtful look, he said, 'We're celebrating, remember? It's only a light wine, and you didn't even drink your sherry.'

That was true, and Kyla wasn't in the least lightheaded. She shrugged and went on eating. The next time Marc refilled the glass she hardly noticed.

Mrs Bridgeway came in carrying two glass sweet dishes, and stopped in the doorway. 'I'm sorry,' she said. 'Am I too early with this?'

'We've been talking,' Marc smiled at her. 'Leave them

on the table, Mrs Bridgeway, and then you can go home if you like. I can fix the coffee.'

'Well, this is cold,' said Mrs Bridgeway. 'Chocolate mousse. I hope you like it, Miss Vernon.'

'Mmm, sounds lovely,' Kyla assured her. 'The whole meal is delicious, Mrs Bridgeway.'

The woman smiled in a pleased way and said goodnight to them both, leaving the sweet dishes on the table. The mousse was covered with a mound of whipped cream and topped with chopped nuts and grated chocolate. When Kyla had finished her fish and put her plate to one side, she looked at the sweet regretfully and said, 'It looks fantastic, but I don't think I could.'

Marc spooned into his, smiling at her. 'You'll have to taste it so that I can tell her how much you enjoyed it. Try it.'

Kyla tried a spoonful. It melted in her mouth, and she ate almost half before she finally put down her spoon. 'I've been greedy,' she said. 'I really couldn't eat another mouthful.'

Marc laughed. 'Finish your wine,' he suggested. 'It will help to wash it down.'

Kyla did so, thinking that in this mood she could almost like him too much. Their earlier tenseness had dissipated over the meal, and he seemed neither angry nor predatory, but relaxed and friendly. Guardedly, she lowered her defences and smiled back at him.

He picked up the wine bottle and motioned to her glass, but she shook her head. He filled his own glass, emptying the bottle, and sat back in his chair, slowly savouring it. 'Are you in a hurry for coffee?' he asked.

'No. Would you like me to make it? And what about these dishes?'

'You can help me if you like,' he said. 'But there won't be much to do. The dishes go in a machine and the coffee will be left nicely perking for us. Yes, I'm shockingly spoiled,' he added, watching the expression on her face. 'Would you believe my sister and I used to do the dishes when we were kids?'

Kyla just smiled and shrugged. Marc finished his wine, tossing back his head and putting the glass down suddenly. He flashed her a brief glance that held a gleam that made her momentarily wary again, then he smiled at her and stood up, stacking the plates together to carry them to the kitchen.

Kyla followed, carrying the bread basket and cruet set, and looked round with interest at a big, old-fashioned kitchen that had been cleverly updated for efficiency without losing its original charm. The stainless steel sink, the big refrigerator and the automatic electric stove had been skilfully blended with colonial-style cupboards and sturdy, practical wooden fittings and furniture. Noting her interest as he stacked the dishes into the under-bench dishwashing machine, Marc asked, 'Would you like a tour of the house?'

'Yes, I would,' she said instantly.

'The bathroom is just across the hall. You can inspect that while I finish in here, if you like. Then I'll show you the rest.'

Tactful, Kyla thought, and fetched her small bag from the sitting room before accepting the offer. The bathroom, like the kitchen, had been modernised with style. She glanced in the oval mirror over the washbasin and freshened her lipstick before returning to the kitchen.

'Coffee first, or later?' asked Marc as she placed her bag on the scrubbed table.

'Later is fine,' she said.

'Okay, let's go.'

There was a small, cosy room furnished as a study, and a glassed-in sun porch opening off that which held a lounging chair, a pile of big cushions and a wall of books. Kyla inspected some of the titles. '*Peter Rabbit*?' she queried, raising her brows.

'My sister's kids,' Marc explained. 'They like to come in here on wet days.'

'I see. Oh, these are yours,' she said positively. He came over to stand beside her as she touched a finger to the spines of a row of thrillers on a top shelf.

'You remembered,' he said, looking down at her. 'Nothing to your taste, here, I'm afraid.'

'You don't know what my taste is.'

'From your spirited defence of romantic novels, I gathered it lay in that direction.'

'Then you gathered wrongly,' she said crisply. 'If you remember, I was generalising on the comparison between men's and women's literary preferences. You were being disparaging about the number of women who prefer romance to tales of murder and violence.'

'Then you don't hanker after a Regency beau to kiss your hand and defend your honour?'

'I don't want anyone to kiss my hand, and my honour—isn't in any need of defending. Actually,' she went on, pointing to some of the titles on the shelf, 'I enjoyed that one—and that. A lot of women, of course, read both kinds of book, as well as others.'

'So you read thrillers,' he said, as they turned away and he led the way back to the long passage. 'And what else?'

Kyla shrugged. 'I've read a few best-sellers,' she said. 'Like everyone. But the books I've enjoyed most have been classics by women writers.'

'Jane Austen and the Brontës?' he said, opening a closed door and motioning her to enter the room as he switched on the light.

'And George Eliot, Elizabeth Gaskell, Fanny Burney, Mary Shelley——' She broke off. 'What a lovely room!'

'It belonged to my parents. They should have had the

front room, but they liked this one—said it was more private.'

'Is this the way it was——'

'When they used it, yes. There's never been a reason to change it.'

The rosewood bed was set off by a white crocheted bedspread over a deep blue lining, a faded floral carpet square covered the floor, and an array of photographs almost covered one wall. Seeing her looking at them, Marc explained, 'The family gallery. Here's my grandfather Marcus.'

'Were you named for him?' she asked, looking at the bearded patriarchal figure with the stiff collar.

'Sort of. I was christened Marc, but it was with old Marcus in mind.'

'And this is your parents' wedding photograph.' She looked with interest at the flowing white dress of the bride and the dark, smoothly handsome face of the man standing with unbending formality beside her. 'And this is——'

She had stopped in front of a studio portrait of a solemn, dark-haired boy of about five, and a smaller girl with a rounded baby face and soft curls.

'Yes, it's me,' Marc grinned. 'With my sister Megan. My mother didn't like that one because I wasn't smiling. I didn't like the photographer. He wanted me to laugh at a bunny rabbit, as he called it, and at five I was convinced it was beneath my dignity.'

Kyla laughed. 'You remember it?'

'Vividly. It was a traumatic experience. To this day I detest having my photograph taken.'

'But you must have had others,' she said. 'Are there any more of you here?'

'No. I refused to allow it.'

'Even as a child?'

His eyes glinted at her. 'Yes,' he said. 'Even as a child,

you see, I got my way. Or, to put it another way, my mother respected my wishes.'

The spare room was next. 'It used to be Meg's,' he told her. It was pretty but had none of the personal charm of the other. Meg had taken the tokens of her own personality with her to her new home, Kyla supposed.

The door of the front room was ajar. Marc pushed it wide and switched on the light, his eyes inviting her in as he stood just inside the door. She swept a cursory glance about the textured wallpaper, the masculine clutter on the dark wood of the old dressing-table, the woven natural wool spread on the wide modern divan bed, and declined with a faint shake of her head.

Marc shrugged, his smile only slightly mocking, and allowed her to lead the way back into the sitting room. It seemed more dimly lit than before, from two soft wall lamps, and she realised that the dining room light had been switched off, making the difference.

'You seem to have a lot of family feeling,' she observed. 'And yet you're not married yourself.'

She sat down in the chair she had taken before, and Marc walked to a cabinet on one wall, taking a handful of records from it. 'My parents set a high standard for marriage,' he explained. 'I made up my mind not to marry until I found a girl who made me care as deeply for her as my father did for my mother.'

That surprised her. She would never have thought him capable of such romanticism.

'What a pity,' she said, as he put a disc on a hidden turn-table and music filtered into the room, 'that you never found her.'

'I'm not in my dotage yet,' he said, turning to face her. 'There's time.'

Thoughtfully, Kyla asked, 'Supposing she doesn't feel the same about you?'

shabby tee-shirts, and wore untidy beards and long hair.

'Kyla—Kyla Vernon,' the first said, looming over her.

'I don't think——' Kyla began coldly, while her heart hammered in trepidation.

The man laughed and said, 'Don't recognise me with the beard, do you? Toby Trench. This is Oliver,' he added, waving vaguely at his companion. Without asking for an invitation he sat down, telling his friend to grab a chair. He nodded casually to Marc, saying, 'Hi—don't mind, do you? Kyla and I were at school together, but I haven't seen her for years. You look great, Kyla. Great. What are you doing in Australia? Great place. I've been here two years. You ...?'

'We're—on holiday,' Kyla managed to say, before he began talking again.

'You'll love it,' Toby said enthusiastically. 'Great place, Sydney—not like that one-horse town we come from, eh, Kyla?'

Kyla smiled stiffly and shook her head. She looked at Marc, but his eyes were on the young man, giving him a narrow-eyed scrutiny. The other man, sitting by Toby, looked into space with a bored expression.

'What have you been doing with yourself, anyway?' Toby asked genially. 'Heard you'd gone up North. Gone up North for a while, eh?' he said meaningfully, leaning closer. 'Most girls come back after six months or so—or nine. But you didn't, did you?'

Kyla paled and saw Marc stiffen and push back his chair. 'Let's go, Kyla,' he said.

She was only too ready to follow him, but Toby grabbed at her arm as she rose, saying anxiously, 'What's the matter, Kyla—I said something wrong? Didn't mean to offend——'

Marc's voice said like a whiplash, '*Let go of my wife.*'

Toby dropped his hand hastily. 'Sorry—your wife? No one told me, mate. No offence—lots of girls go North, doesn't mean a thing——'

He was still apologising as Marc thrust Kyla through the door and into the street outside. He walked so fast she had trouble keeping up with him, but his hand on her arm kept her with him, the fingers digging into her flesh.

'Nice friends you have,' he commented harshly.

'He isn't a friend,' she said. 'We went to the same school, a long time ago. He was quite a nice boy, though, as I remember. He must have been drunk.'

Marc slowed a little. 'Not drunk,' he said grimly.

Kyla looked at him and said, 'Drugs? Oh, that's awful! His poor parents.'

'I don't know what Toby's normal manner is, but his friend was unquestionably stoned out of his mind.'

His face was full of distaste, and his grip on her arm hurt. She said with a small show of spirit, 'It wasn't my fault, Marc!'

'I didn't say it was.'

'Well, you're certainly acting as though I'm to blame in some way!' She reached across and put her hand on his where it still held her arm, and forced him to a halt by stopping herself.

He looked down in surprise and suddenly let her go. 'God! I didn't realise——' he exclaimed. 'You should have said something . . .'

As she turned away and walked on more slowly, he came beside her and said, 'I'm sorry. I wanted to smash his face in, to protect you from his filthy tongue, and now I've hurt you instead.'

Kyla shook her head. 'I'm all right,' she said. 'I'm glad you didn't hit him.'

'It would have given me great satisfaction, but it would

hardly help, to involve you in a brawl. Let's hope we don't come across him again.'

It was ironic, Kyla thought. In Auckland she had once or twice turned her head aside or dodged into a nearby shop or side-street to avoid a familiar face, but further north she had been lucky. She had to cross the Tasman for the constant nightmare fear to be realised, for an unavoidable face to face confrontation with a reminder from the past. She had felt sick when she heard Toby call her name; sick and frightened. She still felt a little sick.

When they reached their hotel, Marc said, 'I need a drink. Come into the bar.'

They sat at a small table and drank slowly and in silence. Kyla played with a cherry on a stick in her empty glass, and Marc asked, 'Would you like another?'

She said no, and then yes, and he cast her an ironic glance and got one for her.

'Would you like to go to a show?' he asked. 'Or a night-club?'

She said, 'All right.'

Marc enquired at the hotel desk and was given a list of places. They took a taxi to King's Cross and admired the spectacular lighted fountain, and Kyla walked quickly past some of the doorways advertising the shows to be seen inside. Once Marc said, 'Don't worry, I'm told the place we're heading for doesn't go in for that sort of thing.'

It was rather a nice place, quietly elegant and probably, Kyla thought, wildly expensive. There was a singer and a small band and a dance floor, and Marc persuaded her to dance with him. She tried to relax in his encircling arms, but it was difficult, and after two dances he pulled her purposefully to him, his lips against her temple, and muttered, 'For God's sake, let go a bit. Put your arms round me.'

Hesitantly she linked her hands behind his neck, but the touch of reined-in temper in his voice hadn't helped, and her body in his arms was as stiff as ever. The evening was rapidly becoming a disaster. Kyla felt both tense and depressed, and Marc seemed to be trying too hard to overcome her mood and his own.

When they entered their room at the hotel again, he shed his jacket and tie and walked over to the window, looking out at the lights and the people who still hurried by in the street below. Kyla used the bathroom and came out wearing her robe over her nightgown. She put away her clothes, and Marc still stood with his back to her at the window. She hesitated, her hand on the belt of her robe, and he turned slowly and came over to her.

She stood very still, but when his hand tipped her face up, her eyes went dark and frightened under the searing intentness of his examination.

Marc's face was hard, and as he took in her expression, his mouth twisted. 'Go to bed,' he said, in a tone of weary disgust. 'Obviously you're not in the mood tonight. I don't feel much like a loving husband myself. I'd probably hurt you in the end.'

He dropped his hand and left her, turning abruptly away and going into the bathroom.

CHAPTER SEVEN

THE following day they did the sightseers' things—crossed the famous bridge across the harbour, admired the fantastic soaring layered wings of the Opera House roof from a distance, and later wandered through some of its rooms, took a ferry boat ride on the harbour and admired the giant span of the bridge again from there. Late in the day they wandered through a green park, read the inscriptions on the monument to war dead, and lazed under a leafy tree, idly watching the crowds hurrying along a distant street.

Marc took Kyla's hand in his and laid it on his knee, idly playing with her fingers and touching his rings on her third finger. He had been rather aloofly pleasant all day, an undemanding and thoughtful companion. And Kyla had tried to match his manner, finding it easier as the day wore on to relax and enjoy herself.

He was looking down at her hand as he touched it, his thumb running over her knuckles, then caressing her palm as he turned it over. There was a faint frown between his brows and his mouth looked stern.

'Marc——' she began.

'Yes?' He didn't look up, and his voice sounded oddly terse.

'You don't—you haven't been wondering if there was something in what Toby said last night, have you—that I might have left home to have a baby?'

'Let's forget about Toby,' he said, dropping her hand and shifting to lie back on his hands. 'He's a fool.'

'You didn't answer my question.'

Marc sat up, staring at her. 'Did it need an answer? Of course I haven't been thinking any such thing! In your case, the idea's ludicrous.'

'Why?'

'My darling, you've never had a love affair in your life—have you?'

'No. But how could you be so certain?'

'For an intelligent girl you ask some very silly questions.'

'Well, you haven't—you don't have any proof, do you?'

Deliberately he said, 'Not yet. I don't need it. I've no doubt there will be sufficient "proof" when the time comes.'

'A lack of evidence isn't always conclusive,' she said huskily. 'Did you know that?'

'I did, as a matter of fact. I wasn't necessarily thinking of the kind of evidence that forms a part of primitive marriage rites. There are more subtle signs that are just as telling. Not always physical ones.'

'You think you know all about me, don't you?' she said, her face troubled.

'Oh, no, I have a lot to find out about you. And there's a certain rather important area of knowledge about each other which we've barely touched as yet.'

Kyla looked down at her hands, and in a moment, one of Marc's reached out to cover them warmly. 'Don't fret about it,' he said. 'Everything doesn't have to happen at once. We've all the time in the world, if you just let things happen naturally. And they will. But only as fast and as far as you want.'

'You're being very patient,' she said quietly.

'I can afford to be. I've got till death us do part. And I don't intend to die for a long time yet.'

'I hope not!'

Marc's arm came round her, holding her close. 'Thank you. I like that touch of terror in your voice. Makes me feel wanted.'

'Beast!' she muttered, her face muffled against his shirt. 'Marc——'

'Mm?' His lips brushed her temple, and as she hesitated, he lifted her face with a hand beneath her chin. 'Don't look so worried,' he said. 'It's going to be all right.'

She tried to speak again, thinking that in this gentle mood he might make it easy for her. But as her lips parted on the words, his mouth claimed hers in a sweet, passionate possession. She lay quietly in his arms, until he lifted his head a little and murmured, 'No response?'

Her lips quivered as she tried to answer him, and he took them again, kissing her unmercifully until she trembled and made a tiny protesting sound in her throat.

'Marc!' she gasped when he finally let her speak. 'There are people——'

'Unfortunately,' he agreed. His eyes held a disconcerting glitter, as he released her. 'It isn't illegal to kiss my wife in a public place, though.'

Kyla didn't answer, standing up to smooth her hair and shake out her skirt. She avoided his eyes, knowing he was watching her intently.

'Let's go back to the hotel,' he said.

But when he took her in his arms in the intimacy of their room, and pulled her down on the bed, she was suddenly inhibited again, her fears and doubts swamping the wakening delight of her senses. Eventually he rolled away and stood up, turning from her while he did up the buttons on his shirt and thrust back the dark disorder of his hair.

Kyla swung her feet to the floor, her back to him as she sat on the bed and put her hands to her hair. She had stopped him when he tried to take out the pins, but a few loose strands brushed her nape, and she quickly combed them and pinned them back into place, then straightened her blouse, tucking it firmly into the waistband of her skirt.

'You look as fresh as a daisy,' said Marc as she trod into her shoes. 'No one would ever know you'd even been kissed.'

His tone made it less than a compliment, and she cast him a cautious look without answering.

'I'm going out,' he said. 'Do you want to come?'

Kyla shook her head, having a distinct impression that at this moment her company was not welcome. 'Will you be long?' she asked.

'I don't know. Will you mind eating alone if I'm not back for dinner?'

She shook her head. She did mind, but wouldn't dare say so. He was very controlled at the moment, but beneath the surface she knew very well there was something highly charged and dangerous. When he had gone, it was minutes before she could force her tense muscles to relax.

She had a snack in their room, and went to bed early, only to lie awake worrying until she heard Marc come in. Then, strangely, she was asleep before he came out of the bathroom.

The next day they visited the Taronga Park zoo, and she was grateful that Marc's mood was tender and teasing, dispelling the emotional atmosphere of the previous evening. They laughed at the cuddly koala bears, stared at the kangaroos and Kyla, at least, shuddered at the snakes. Marc showed a total fascination with the bright, beautifully patterned skins and sinuous movements of the creatures, but Kyla was repelled. 'I'm glad to have seen them,' she admitted later. 'But once is enough.'

Much more to her liking were the tiny squirrels jumping and darting about among the trees that lined the paths between the enclosures. They were more of a novelty than the elephants and tigers, which could be seen in zoos back home.

Marc hired a car, and they spent a few days driving

about, across Sidney Nolan landscapes in browns and reds and greys, stretching away into infinity across a vast land, and once glimpsed a family of koalas scrambling about in a grove of magnificent blue-grey gumtrees. They visited the Blue Mountains and gasped at vistas of rugged, bush-covered terrain, and took a boat to the mouth of the Hawkesbury, leaning over the side in fascination to watch a flotilla of brilliant, umbrella-shaped, colourfully spotted jellyfish floating along beside the craft.

On their last day they found a quiet, almost deserted beach not far from the city and dared a quick bracing swim in the surf, before they dressed and strolled along the sand to where an outcrop of rock gave shelter from a cooling breeze, and in a nearby tree a kookaburra intermittently gave his harsh, mocking laugh.

Kyla sat with her arms clasped round her raised knees, clad in casual jeans. Marc lay on his elbow beside her and a little to the rear, his eyes on her as she idly watched the rolling of the sea and the spuming crests flinging on to the shore.

A cloud scudded away from the sun, and Kyla raised her face to its warmth, her eyes closing.

'Kyla,' Marc said softly, 'take down your hair.'

Kyla didn't move, her body growing tense in stillness. 'No,' she said.

'Please.' His voice was still soft, coaxing and a little amused.

'I'm sorry, Marc. No.'

He sat up suddenly and came behind her, laughing a little. 'Then I'll do it,' he said, teasing her. His fingers fumbled with the pins, and Kyla pulled away from him. Still laughing, he grabbed at her, hauling her firmly back against his chest, his hands determined as one of them returned to her head.

Kyla twisted, panting, in his arms, and as he tried to contain her struggles, raked her nails down his cheek and neck.

Startled, Marc drew back, but when she pushed out of his hold, he pulled her back with hands that no longer held any gentleness, twisting her wrists behind her with one hand while the other tugged the pins roughly from her hair and scattered them on the sand, ignoring her angry, gasping protests and the frantic attempts she was making to twist away from him. When her hair was soft and dishevelled about her shoulders, he grabbed a painful swatch of it in one hand and pushed her backwards on to the sand. She glimpsed a dark, savage fury in his face before it blotted out the sun and his mouth ravaged hers in a hard, merciless kiss that went on and on. She felt his hand tugging at the buttons of her shirt, and moaned deep in her throat.

His hand found her breast and claimed it in a firm, insolent caress. Kyla realised her hands had been freed, and beat them against his shoulders and face in frantic fear and anger. He grunted, lifted his head and grabbed her flailing hands, forcing them down in his to lie flat and helpless against the sand. His leg was thrown across both of hers, his body pinned hers, hard and heavy against her softness. She was helpless, her anger negligible in the face of his easy strength.

'Wildcat!' he muttered. 'What now?'

'Let me go!' she spat at him like the wild creature he had called her. '*I hate you, Marc!*'

'Really?' His eyes flicked over her flushed face, and moved to linger on the soft flesh scarcely covered by a wisp of bra beneath her open blouse. His eyes moved back to hers and held them. 'I want you,' he said flatly.

She went pale, her throat locking and her eyes appalled. '*No!*' she said in a shocked whisper. Then, her voice rising a little, '*No!*'

Her voice was cut off by his mouth, his kiss bruising

her lips with its force. Then suddenly she was free, and she opened dazed eyes to see Marc striding to the water's edge, standing there with his clenched hands thrust into his pockets, looking out over the wild water.

She sat up slowly, and began frantically searching the sand for her hairpins, her hands trembling as she tried desperately to restore some order to her hair. It was damp from the sea, and grains of sand clung stubbornly to the dampness. She sobbed with frustration and disgust, and angrily wiped tears from her face with the back of her hand, finding it gritty against her skin. One of the buttons from her blouse lay on the beach, and she bit her lip fiercely as she retrieved it and did up the remainder with shaking fingers.

When Marc came striding back across the sand she was standing up, still fiddling despairingly with her hair, fingers anxiously smoothing and tucking, knowing that it still looked untidy and full of sand.

His look as he watched her futile efforts was almost compassionate.

'Are you all right?' he asked.

'Yes.' She couldn't say more, couldn't look at him.

Marc's mouth was grimly set. 'I'm not going to apologise,' he said evenly. 'You asked for what you got.'

Kyla shivered, and a small, smothered sound forced its way from her throat to her lips, like a whimper of anguish.

Marc moved quickly, his hand coming out to touch her, a quick frown in his eyes, and Kyla shied away like a startled animal, avoiding him.

'Can we go back to the car?' she said. 'My comb is there.'

The comb helped a little, but back at the hotel she washed her hair thoroughly under the shower, towelled it with considerable force, and combed it ruthlessly before pinning it up again. When she came out of the bathroom

Marc was sitting in a chair reading. He didn't look up, and she hastily moved her eyes away from the vivid scratch marks that crossed his jawline and disappeared into the collar of his shirt.

She was surprised when he told her they were going out. 'Wear something dressy,' he told her. 'We're going to a show.'

She put a bare-necked, dark synthetic dress and threw a fringed shawl over her shoulders. The place Marc took her to had a club atmosphere, and the entertainment was music and dancing. Most of the dancers were female, and the costumes were glittering, sexy and in many cases extremely scanty. Looking away in embarrassment from the suggestive gyrations of a girl on the small stage, she glanced at Marc and saw that he was watching impassively, leaning back a little in his chair, apparently relaxed and unaware of her beside him.

The girl was moving off the stage into the audience, swaying her hips in time to the music, flirting with some of the male patrons, flipping a tie here, raising a laugh by smoothing her fingers over a bald head there. Kyla tensed as she neared their table and stood smiling provocatively down at Marc. He tipped his head back, and Kyla felt her nails dig into her palms as she saw his leisurely, amused and appreciative inspection of the dancer's luscious figure. The girl's hand reached out and touched the marks on his neck, her lips pursing in a parody of commiseration, and Marc caught her hand in his and smiled before he let her move on.

Kyla discovered a desperate desire to leave, but as Marc turned his head to look at her, she met his eyes with a sudden, certain knowledge that he would not be leaving until he was good and ready, and that he meant to keep her here, too. She wasn't sure what the hard look in his eyes meant, but that he was waiting for some reaction from her, she knew. He was not going to take her back to the hotel, and she wouldn't give him the satisfaction of refusing by asking him to do so. She sat for the rest of the long evening waiting for him to make a move, her eyes for the most part fixed on the empty glass before her.

They took a taxi back to the hotel, and Kyla looked out at the flashing advertising lights, with a cool profile turned to her husband, all the way. Neither of them spoke until they were in their room, then Marc shrugged off his dark jacket and enquired, 'Did you enjoy the show?'

'No.' She was sure he knew it, and she wouldn't pretend.

'Why not?' he asked, pulling off his tie and beginning to undo the buttons on his shirt.

'I think you know that,' she said. 'It was the kind of thing that appeals to men.'

'A lot of women enjoy it, too,' he said. 'We could have gone to a male strip show, but I didn't think that would be your scene.'

'You know very well it isn't,' she said in a choked voice, and went into the bathroom, closing the door with a brisk snap.

She washed, and brushed her teeth vigorously, then moved back to the other room. Marc was lying on his bed, hands behind his head. He didn't move as Kyla went to her own bed and took out her nightgown. She slipped out of her shoes, put away a few things that were lying about, and finally said, 'Don't you want the bathroom?'

'Later,' he said lazily, his eyes following her.

Kyla hesitated, standing beside the nightgown laid on her bed. Behind her, Marc suddenly stood up, said, 'Want some help?' and then she felt his hand sliding down the zipper at the back of her dress.

Startled, she jumped, whirled round and backed from

him. 'No,' she said, and picked up the nightgown, moving away. 'If you don't want the bathroom, I'll get undressed in there.'

'You'll get undressed here,' said Marc.

Her eyes dilated, and she bolted for the bathroom door. But somehow Marc got there first, and was standing with his back to it. 'Here.' He said it implacably, very quiet.

'I'm not one of those showgirls!' Kyla flashed at him.

'No, you're my wife. Married people don't hide their bodies from each other. They don't go into the bathroom every time they change their clothes. I meant it when I said we'd take things gradually, Kyla. But we have to start somewhere.'

His tone had softened a little, but Kyla was too angry to care. 'If you wanted a strip-tease show,' she snapped, 'you should have gone to one! Alone.'

A muscle flickered in his cheek. He reached out his hands and quite gently eased her dress from her shoulders. Her hands, clutching the nightgown in front of her, prevented it from slipping further. He said, 'Will I help you, or will you finish it yourself?'

She backed away, then turned to return to her bed, dropping the nightgown on it. Without looking round, she stood with her back to him, and eased the dress right down until she could step out of it. Her hands fumbled behind her for the catch of her bra, and she dropped it on the bed. Her mouth was dry and her heart thudding, as she stood in her brief panties, picked up the nightgown and dropped it over her head. Then she turned to face Marc with her head up and her eyes blazing hatred.

He wasn't looking at her. He still stood in front of the bathroom door, with his head turned from her. Kyla sat down on the bed. She knew he hadn't watched her at all. She slipped into the bed, and he asked, 'Have you finished?'

'Yes.'

He turned then and gave her a faint smile. 'It wasn't so bad, was it?' he asked her.

Then before she could answer, he opened the door behind him and went into the bathroom.

Kyla was restless long after Marc appeared to have gone to sleep in the darkness. Tomorrow they would be flying home, their honeymoon completed, and their marriage— incomplete. She knew that was her fault, and that Marc was being remarkably forbearing for a man who was used to having his own way in everything. And yet, although he could be tender and understanding, he was capable of sudden violence that frightened her. There were times when she was ready to confide in him, but then the fear held her back.

She supposed she *had* asked for what she had got, today. It had not been necessary for her to react so strongly— no wonder he had been angry. But she wished she knew why he had chosen that show to take her to. Had it been another punishment? Had he wanted to show her that there were women who were not as inhibited, not as cold as his wife, women who enjoyed the attentions of men like himself? And who could bring him pleasure, even if it was only the pleasure of looking at them?

She remembered the way the girl in that place had touched him and looked at him, and how she had obviously enjoyed his lazy admiration. For a fantastic moment she envied the girl, who could confidently, serenely, encourage men to look at her like that. She had never had that confidence, never would have. Something in her, perhaps, some vital aspect of her femininity, was crippled.

Returning to New Zealand was oddly disorientating. Everything looked different, although they had only been away for a week. The trees were incredibly green, the houses tremendously colourful, the grass under the early winter rains lush and rich, too intensely emerald to be real. As they drove north, passing almost deserted beaches, long sweeps of white-gold sand, and speeding along beside neatly fenced farms, then winding through the hills among patches of manuka, fronded ferns and tall native bush, Kyla realised with a rush of pleasure how very beautiful it was. When from the top of the last hill she looked down into hazy distance and saw the lowland, the distant sea and the flare of the Marsden Point oil refinery towers, she felt a sense of homecoming so intense that she took a quick breath and let it out in a small sigh.

Marc glanced at her. 'Nearly home,' he said. 'Are you glad or sorry?'

'Glad,' she said instantly.

He smiled wryly. 'Well, it wasn't much of a honeymoon,' he said.

'About that,' she said carefully, 'I'm sorry. But I enjoyed Sydney. Thank you for taking me there.'

He drove on in silence and she asked, 'Was it a total loss for you?'

'No. I enjoyed it too, in spite of the moments of—frustration. And I expect we've learned a little more about each other, haven't we? So it can't be counted as a loss. As a honeymoon it was a little unconventional, but if you enjoyed yourself, at least part of the object of the exercise was fulfilled.'

By the time they reached Marc's house, Kyla had begun to be nervous again. He hauled their cases out of the car while she opened the door with the key he had handed her, and when she stepped back he walked past her with a suitcase in either hand, one hers and one his own. He took them both into the big front bedroom that had been redecorated before the wedding, and said casually as he went back to the car for more luggage, 'You can start unpacking if you like. I've left you plenty of room in the wardrobe.'

He was making it plain that he expected her to share that room with him as they had planned. She went into it slowly, and the first thing that caught her eyes was the big new double bed covered with a fringed brocade spread. One sliding door of the new built-in wardrobe was open, and she saw a man's coat sleeve and a row of empty hangers.

When Marc brought in two smaller bags and put them on the bed, she turned to him, her face full of objections. But she took one look at his closed expression and the hard glow in his grey-blue eyes and knew he wouldn't stand for one. They had been sharing a room, and now they were going to share a bed. Marc had made the decision, and she resented it, but there was no complaint she could make. It was one of the small habits of married people that he was forcing her to accept, one of their gradual steps to a full married life of their own. She said nothing, and he went out again without comment.

Suddenly impatient with herself, she threw open the cases and began unpacking feverishly. Half her clothes were already hanging up when Marc came in and asked, 'Would you like a drink? Hot or alcoholic?'

'I'll finish this first,' she said. 'Do you want me to unpack for you?'

'You're my wife, not my servant,' he said, and threw his own case on the bed, pulling at the straps which bound it.

He finished before she did, and lay on the bed watching her move about the room. 'What shall I do with the empty bags?' she asked him.

'Leave them. I'll put them away later. Come here.'

Kyla moved slowly over to the bed, and he put out his hand and held hers.

'Closer,' he said, and gave her hand a tug, pulling her down beside him. One of her shoes fell to the floor, and he sat up, removed the other and drew her into his arms to lie close to him, her head against his shoulder. 'It's okay,' he said soothingly. 'Just stay there.'

Gradually she relaxed against the warmth of his body, and slowly he began to stroke her arm, then his hand moved to her throat and slipped to the back of her head. She felt the fingers touching her hair tug experimentally at one of the pins that held it; and she stiffened. The fingers stilled, then moved again to caress her neck, touching the lobes of her ears, wandering across her cheek and pressing on her lower lip until her mouth parted. Then he turned a little and kissed her softly on the mouth. Kyla made a random, reflexive movement with her hand, and encountered the tensed muscles of his arm beneath his cotton shirt. Tentatively her fingers explored it, running over the hard male contours. The pressure of his mouth on hers became deeper and his hand began to stroke her body gently, moving with a slow deliberation from her breast to her thigh and back again. Kyla moved her hand to his shoulder and raised her other arm, to put both arms about him. Her mouth opened sweetly for him as he silently demanded it, and then he moved on the bed, pulling her closer and thrust his thigh between hers.

Her sudden protest was silent but unmistakable. Her hands fell back on the bed, curled into fists. Her body arched and stiffened and her head tried to push back into the pillow behind her.

She heard a stifled curse as Marc rolled away from her, lying on his back and breathing hard, and she huddled on the bed with her back to him, her teeth sinking into the knuckles of one hand.

After what seemed a long time, he said wearily, 'Come and have that drink.'

Kyla got off the bed without looking at him, and he stood aside at the door to let her go first into the kitchen at the end of the long passage.

He made coffee and she got the cups. They spoke to each other politely, and drank the coffee thankfully because it saved them talking to each other.

Kyla picked up the cups afterwards, and Marc said abruptly that he had some telephone calls to make, and went into the wide hall where the telephone was. She heard his voice speaking decisively as she rinsed out the cups they had used.

She felt travel-weary and stale, and decided to have a shower and change. She stripped off and showered in the bathroom, protecting her hair with a plastic shower cap, and when she had finished she wrapped a cotton robe about her and returned to the bedroom. Marc was still speaking on the telephone, and as she passed him he glanced over her almost indifferently. But she knew that his eyes were following her as she entered the bedroom.

She put on a long fine woollen skirt and a silk, long-sleeved shirt-style blouse, then brushed out her hair, re-pinned it and put on fresh light make-up. She was only filling in time, really. She heard the ping as the receiver of the telephone was replaced, and as Marc strolled into the room she got up from the dressing table and said, 'I'll make us something to eat.'

The day was turning chilly and she opened a tin of soup to start the meal. She found a casserole of veal in the refrigerator; Mrs Bridgeway must have made it ready for their homecoming, as well as stocking the refrigerator with milk, eggs and some fresh vegetables.

'Can I help?' Marc's voice enquired from the doorway.

'It's all right, I can manage,' she said. 'Mrs Bridgeway has been very efficient, as usual.'

'That's what I pay her for,' he said. She thought he

would go away, but he didn't, he stayed lounging in the doorway watching her, until she said nervously, 'You can get the table ready, if you like.'

He set out plates and cutlery, then found a bottle of wine and put that on the table as well. When they sat down to their soup, he poured some into two glasses and raised his to her silently.

Kyla tried to smile, but his face was hard and rather watchful, not tender at all, so she raised her own glass and sipped quickly at the wine to hide her agitation.

He kept filling her glass and she kept drinking from it, throughout the meal. She felt a mild glow on her cheeks and when she stood up to clear away her knees felt odd, but it soon passed. She realised she had probably drunk more wine than ever before in her life, but thought vaguely that it might help ...

They sat with their coffee in the sitting room and Kyla recalled the first time she had had dinner here with Marc. It seemed ages ago, but wasn't really. Marc put on a record, not dance tunes this time, but a selection of light classics, and she said, 'That's nice.'

She leaned her head against the high back of the chair, moving it quickly as she saw him make a movement. He was only putting his cup on a side table but he glanced up at her enquiringly as he settled back.

Kyla put a hand to her hair, feeling something tugged out of place with the sudden turning of her head, and Marc asked, as she smoothed it, 'Have you always had long hair?'

'I had it cut short once, when I was seventeen. But it blew about in the wind and got into my eyes. It's really easier to manage this way.'

'Have you never worn it loose?'

'Not since I let it grow again. I don't like it round my face. It gets too untidy.'

His mouth quirked in an odd, knowing smile. His eyes moved over her and he said, 'That's a pretty skirt.'

She looked down at the pattern of small white daisies on a dark blue ground, and said, 'It's warm. I don't need stockings with it.'

Marc smiled again, more definitely. Kyla realised he was laughing at her and felt a surge of resentment. She put down her cup with a tiny crash, and Marc's eyes narrowed in amusement.

'You're not a romantic, are you, Kyla?' he said, on a softly jeering note.

'Are you?' she countered.

'That depends on the circumstances.'

'Well, perhaps that goes for everyone,' she said.

'Including you?'

Kyla shrugged.

The record came to a stop, and he got up and changed it. She recognised the sound of the music they had danced to once before, and Marc came over to her, took her hands and pulled her out of the chair.

Perhaps because she was trying too hard to relax and get into the mood of that other evening when he had taken her in his arms like this and made her dance with him, she found herself going rigid, following the steps but without any spontaneous sense of being with the music. It was better in the faster numbers, when he let her dance away from him, and when he put his arm about her waist again she felt a little more relaxed.

His arms closed about her, pulling her close to him. Kyla misstepped and he stopped, still holding her. She knew he was going to kiss her, and drew a deep, shuddering breath in anticipation.

His arms tightened almost unbearably, and she closed her eyes. Then suddenly she was free, swaying dizzily with the suddenness of it. And Marc had turned away from her, going to the record player to switch it off. The silence seemed louder than the music.

'I'm sure you're tired,' he said. 'You'd better go to bed.'

'Yes,' she said. 'Goodnight.'

He threw her a quick, enigmatic glance and didn't reply. In the bedroom, Kyla closed the door, walked to the stool before the dressing table and sat down, pressing her hands to her eyes.

This was impossible. Marc had said they would go slowly, but every time he touched her she seemed more tense. She couldn't help it, and the more she tried to overcome it the worse the problem became. They couldn't go on like this.

She looked up into the mirror at the sound of the door opening behind her. Marc stood there, closing the door and standing against it. He had undone the top buttons of his shirt, and the brown line of his throat looked taut, as though his jaw was tightly clenched above it. His eyes found hers in the mirror.

'I won't wait for ever,' he said quietly. 'And this marriage is never going to work without some sort of effort from you.'

'I know.'

His eyes held hers and then he began to come slowly across the room. Kyla held her back straight, and raised her hands to her hair. Marc stopped a few feet behind her when she began to slide out the pins one by one and place them on the dressing table before her.

When she had finished, she sat for moment with her head bowed, the soft hair falling over her shoulders and screening her face. Then she began to undo her blouse with shaking fingers. She pulled the blouse from the band of her skirt and stood up to face Marc as she drew it off and dropped it on the stool. Without looking at him, she pulled open the hooks at the waist of the skirt, and with her fingers on the zip fastener, she said in an unsteady whisper, 'Please help me, Marc.'

His hands reached out and fastened on her arms painfully, dragging her against him. Her mouth parted on a gasp of pain and fear, and as her head fell back with the force of his grip, he kissed her, but not gently. She recoiled from the hard, bruising pressure of his lips, and as she dragged her mouth from his, his hands moved to her back. His fingers on her skin felt strange and hard, and she dropped her head against his shoulder, biting her lower lip.

His hand was moving over her back, and when he ran his thumb over the clasp of her bra, she held her breath. But then his hand moved back to her waist as he spoke in her ear.

'Do you want me to make love to you, Kyla?'

Her hands were flat against his chest, her forehead rested on the skin exposed by the open shirt. She nodded her head, and whispered, 'Yes.'

One of his hands moved and he hooked his thumb under the strap of her bra, pulling it down. His fingers pushed the flimsy cup down further, and closed over her breast. Kyla closed her eyes and turned her head away. She felt shocked and violated, the touch of his fingers strange and intrusive. She was aware of a faint, pleasant sensual stirring, but in spite of it her flesh seemed to shrink from him.

'You want me?' Marc said with low insistence.

'Yes,' she repeated desperately, her voice muffled against his shirt.

'Say it.'

Oh, please, can't we just get it over with before I lose my courage? Kyla thought frantically. Maybe afterwards she could talk to him, tell him . . .

'Say it,' Marc repeated implacably.

'I—want you,' she murmured, shivering in his arms.

His hand shifted violently, raking into her hair and dragging her head back so that he could look into her eyes. The fright and pain in them increased as she saw the blazing anger in his.

'You liar!' he muttered between his teeth. 'Damn you, Kyla! I want a warm, loving woman in my arms, not a sacrificial victim!'

'I'm sorry!' she whispered miserably.

Abruptly, he let her go. 'Are you?' he gritted. 'That's nice to know,' he added with blatant sarcasm.

She stood with her face averted from him, pulling the strap he had displaced back on to her shoulder, her arms crossed in front of her with her hair falling over her wrists.

She heard him say, 'I'll sleep in the other room,' and then the door snapped shut behind him.

CHAPTER EIGHT

KYLA was glad she had the shop to go to every day. At least while she was kept busy there, the problem of her marriage remained temporarily at bay. After two weeks, Marc was still sleeping in the spare room, leaving her in the new double bed alone. He seemed to have withdrawn from her in other ways, too. He never attempted to make love to her, even mildly, and when he spoke to her it was in the tone of a courteous stranger. They shared a house, and usually travelled together to work, to conserve petrol, and sometimes they talked about the news of the day or discussed a new book or a piece of music, but it was all on the surface. Marc asked her about the shop, and she told him the grass had grown and the playing area was in daily use, that the twins were enjoying living in the little flat, and that profits had risen slightly. She asked about Nathans, and he said the export market was growing and that they hoped to expand the Auckland office next year. It was all very civilised and Kyla was desperately unhappy.

After her one disastrous attempt at taking the initiative, she dared not try again; the next move would have to come from Marc. Sometimes she thought he had lost interest, and fear gripped her as she wondered if he would want to end their marriage. But now and then she caught his eyes on her with a flame of desire lambent in their depths, and she looked away quickly, a tiny frisson of some unidentifiable emotion making her tense her muscles to hide it.

One morning she arrived at the shop to find the door unlocked, and when she pushed it open, Hazel came hurrying to meet her.

Surprised, Kyla said, 'Hello—you're early.'

'The girls called me,' Hazel explained. 'It's Sara——'

'What is it?' Kyla took in Hazel's white face. 'What's happened to her?'

'She's here.' Hazel led the way to the foot of the staircase, where Janet was hovering anxiously over her white-faced twin, who lay awkwardly with her head against the bottom stair. 'I think—her leg's broken,' Janet said.

'An ambulance is on its way,' Hazel explained, her eyes worried, and her face determinedly calm. 'Janet, would you watch out for it—show them where to come?'

She held her daughter's hand, and Kyla crouched beside them, feeling helpless. 'How did it happen?' she asked.

Sara tried to smile. 'My new shoes, I guess. And the fact I was going to be late for work—oh, Mum, will you ring them? Tell them what's happened?'

'I will,' Kyla offered, and moved quickly to the phone. The ambulance arrived shortly afterwards, and Kyla sent Hazel off with it to the hospital.

It was nearly noon before Hazel returned, smiling with relief and ready to regale Kyla with the whole story. The new shoes had very high heels, the stairs were dark and narrow, and Sara's unwise haste had precipitated the inevitable accident. Her leg was in plaster and she had a painful cracked rib, but would be home the following day.

'Home,' Hazel said firmly. 'Not here. I'm afraid they'll have to give up the flat, Kyla. I won't let Janet stay alone. Besides, I'm pretty sure she won't want to be away from her twin at the moment. Those two are very close to each other.'

The girls insisted on returning the key, although Kyla assured them she would keep the flat vacant if they wanted to return when Sara was fully recovered.

'No, you take the key,' said Hazel. 'No favours, please, for us. I don't want my girls taking advantage.'

'They wouldn't be!' Kyla assured her, but she took the key and hung it in the hall of Marc's house on the handsome brass-bound leather key rack that the Wrights had given them for a wedding present.

She still felt that the house was Marc's house. He treated her, she felt, as though she was a favoured guest. Mrs Bridgeway still did the bulk of the housework and cooking, and although Kyla had no particular desire to take on running a house as well as a business, it underlined the fact that as a wife she made very little impact.

So when Marc mentioned that he wanted to give a dinner party for some business friends, and asked if she would prefer to make the arrangements, or leave it to Mrs Brideway, she thankfully accepted the task.

She did without Mrs Bridgeway, except for some help in the afternoon with the preparation, and the meal for ten people was an unqualified success. Kyla accepted the compliments with a pleased glow of satisfaction, and Marc fielded congratulations on his wife's talents with marked urbanity.

The guests stayed late, and Kyla found herself fending off fulsome compliments and unwelcome, explicit glances from one of the men, Duncan Brewster, whose wife kept giving him helpless, resigned looks across the room.

Marc appeared not to notice, she was thankful to see. One or two of the other women gave her sympathetic looks, and later one of them said, as Kyla went with her to the bedroom to fetch her jacket, 'Duncan's quite a nice fellow, really, but a menace when he's had a few. You'd think he'd know better than to try it on with a new bride. Anyway, thanks for a lovely dinner, Kyla. You and Marc must come and eat with us, some time.'

'Thank you. That would be nice.'

The other woman said, 'I mean it. After our daughter's wedding, though. To which you will be receiving an invitation very soon, by the way. She's only eighteen, but—well, these days, if you don't give them permission they just live together, anyway. And he's a nice lad. Maybe they'll be okay, with our help.'

Kyla liked Kate Salmon, and when the promised wedding invitation arrived, surprised Marc by being eager to attend. His eyebrows rising a little, he said, 'All right, if you like. They say every woman loves a wedding, but I thought you might be an exception.'

'Don't you want to go?' she asked. 'The Salmons are your friends.'

'Would it surprise you to know that I'm off weddings at the moment?'

'You mean you're "off" marriage?' Kyla queried in a low voice.

'If you like. Ours isn't exactly a shining example, is it?'

Kyla looked at him, not knowing what to say.

Impatiently, he turned away. 'Forget it,' he said shortly. 'Do you think something in your shop will do for a present for these two?'

'I'll pick out something special for them,' she promised evenly. Perhaps she should have insisted on discussing their marriage, perhaps she was a coward not to have done so. They couldn't go on as they were for ever. But Marc's harsh, forbidding expression warned her off.

The eighteen-year-old bride looked beautiful and touchingly young in a slim white dress with a floating, traditional veil, and Kyla, torn by old regrets, found tears standing in her eyes as the girl exchanged her vows with the nervous young man at her side. She felt Marc's sardonic eyes on her, and stared fiercely at the flower-laden altar before the bridal couple, determined not to let the tears fall.

The formal reception was kept mercifully to a reasonable length by short speeches and a minimum of toasts, and the invitation to come back to the bride's parents' house afterwards was reinforced personally by Kate Salmon, who adjured them to be sure and come. 'Otherwise we'll be stuck with Bill's boring relatives!' she hissed at them as she left them to speak to someone else.

'We can't refuse,' said Kyla, as Marc looked at her questioningly.

He shrugged and said resignedly, 'Okay, let's go.'

At the house the party was more informal, and Kyla soon found Kate in the kitchen, and was happy to be roped in to help make endless cups of tea and wash glasses continuously being emptied in the other rooms.

'Thank you, Kyla, you angel!' Kate smiled on one of her flying trips to collect clean glasses and replenish bowls of nuts and potato crisps. 'But you mustn't be stuck here all the time. Come out and join the party.'

'Soon,' Kyla promised, and Kate withdrew with her hands full of glasses and bowls.

'Need some help?' a male voice asked, and Duncan Brewster was suddenly beside her, a teatowel in his hand.

She didn't need it, and didn't want his help, but there was nothing to do but thank him and go on washing glasses for him to dry. She and Marc had spoken to him briefly at the reception, and he had made one or two joking remarks about the married state and their own recent wedding, which Marc had countered with bland replies. He was even more talkative now, and she deduced he had drunk rather a lot of alcohol.

In a hurry to finish what she was doing and get away from his unwelcome company, she hastened too much, and a glass slipped from her hand and crashed to the floor. They both stooped to pick up the pieces. Duncan smiled at her and then suddenly slid an insinuating hand down her arm. Kyla recoiled, and Duncan said, 'I'll do it, love. Just hand me that brush and shovel in the corner, there.'

Maybe it had been an accidental touch, she told herself as she obeyed. Perhaps she was being stupidly hypersensitive.

She turned back to the sink while he swept up the glass and tipped it into the rubbish bin by the outside door. 'All fixed,' he said. 'How about a kiss for being a good boy?'

He was behind her, sliding his arms about her waist, and Kyla jerked into rigidity, wanting to scream, claw at him and run.

She stopped herself with an effort. He was only a rather pathetic drunk making a mild pass, and she should be able to handle this without getting hysterical about it. She said, 'No, Duncan,' and tried to move his hands away. But hers were slippery with soapy water, and he tightened his hold, nuzzling at her cheek.

His breath was beery, and Kyla felt nauseated. She turned her face away, and he said, 'Aw, don't be like that, Kyla.' He pulled her round to face him and fastened his mouth on hers.

He was surprisingly strong, and he had wrapped his arms about her in a bear-like grip, trapping both of hers. She moved her head back, trying to escape the suffocation of his damp mouth, but he followed, and the sink bench was at her back so that she could scarcely move.

'*What the hell*——!' Marc's sharp voice ripped into the room, and suddenly she was free, and Duncan, breathing heavily, and red-faced, was saying placatingly, 'Just a bit of fun, Marc. You know how it is at weddings.'

Kyla was gripping the bench with both hands behind her. She felt sick and her legs were trembling. Her heart turned over as she looked at Marc. He looked ready to murder someone. 'Don't make a fuss, darling,' she said quickly. 'Duncan's in the party spirit, that's all. He—we were just fooling around.'

His look at her held a faint hint of incredulity. Slowly he said, 'Speaking of the party, Kate sent me to bring you back to it. You've been hiding in here long enough.'

As she went towards him, he put out a hand and captured her wrist, holding it in a bone-breaking grip as they moved into the hall.

'You're hurting me!' she protested, and Marc looked down with a strange glitter in his eyes and said, 'Too bad.'

But he let her go, and pushed her ahead of him into the living room where most of the guests were gathered round a piano, having a lusty old-fashioned sing-song. Kate came up to her and whispered, 'I saw Duncan heading for the kitchen, and sent Marc in. I thought you might need rescuing.'

Kyla smiled a little wanly. She had an uneasy feeling that it was a case of out of the frying pan and into something much worse. Relieved though she had been to see her husband enter the kitchen, his manner was hardly reassuring. Who was going to rescue her from him?

He, too, seemed to be drinking rather more heavily than he usually did, although she couldn't see that it made any difference to him. His hand was rock-steady and his voice perfectly clear. He had his arm about her waist, clamping her to his side, but he scarcely looked at her. When the bride and groom left, he stood with her on the outskirts of the cheering, waving crowd of well-wishers, and immediately afterwards said, 'Thank God that's over. We'll get away soon.'

But it was not quite that easy. Brent Salmon said, 'I've got something to show you before you go, Marc. I know you'll appreciate it. Come and see——'

He handed Marc a piece of polished kauri gum, palest gold in colour, just the size of a man's palm. Inside the translucent, smooth surface was a perfectly preserved blue-winged butterfly, caught when the gum had oozed from the parent tree in an ancient forest.

'What do you think of that?' Brent asked.

'It's a beautiful piece,' Marc answered. 'Where did you get it?'

'An old aunt of mine who died. Part of the estate came to me, and I made sure I got this. It is a good sample, isn't it? And genuine, not faked.'

'One of the best I've seen,' Marc agreed, holding the piece up to the light. 'There isn't a flaw in it.'

He held it out to Kyla, but she shook her head, not wanting to touch it. Kauri gum was beautiful, fascinating stuff, from the rough, milky lumps of the stuff in its raw state to polished pieces like this in shades ranging from clear pale amber to deep golden bronze. Leaves and mosses found embedded in it were pretty and interesting. But this piece, in spite of its undoubted beauty, repelled her.

'Don't you like butterflies?' Brent asked curiously.

'Yes,' she said. 'But not—imprisoned, like that.'

'That's a funny way of putting it,' Brent laughed. 'It's been dead for hundreds of years, you know.'

'I know. It's lovely, Brent. But I don't want to touch it.'

'Kyla sympathises with the butterfly,' said Marc, his voice tinged with mockery. He handed back the gum, and took her arm firmly as they left the room.

When they reached home, she asked, 'Do you want to eat?'

'I've had plenty,' he said. 'There was enough food there to feed an army.'

'Yes. And drink.' Her eyes were following him as he crossed the sitting room to the drinks cupboard, and took out a bottle and a glass.

'Is that a hint?' he asked, turning to her.

'No.' She had been thinking of Duncan, but it did occur

to her to wonder why Marc needed still more stimulation now.

But he put down the glass without filling it and came over to her. She was sitting in one of the comfortable chairs, and had kicked off her shoes. She watched him warily until he stopped just in front of her.

'You feel like that butterfly, don't you?' he said. 'Trapped for ever.'

'You're being—imaginative,' she said.

'Am I? Was I being imaginative when I saw you in a Hollywood clinch with Duncan?'

'I couldn't stop him,' she protested. 'You surely don't think I *invited* that?'

'You didn't seem to be objecting very strongly—if at all.'

'*For heaven's sake!*' Kyla stood up angrily, but before she could turn away he caught her by the arms. 'Let go!' she stormed at him, pushing against his chest.

'What's happened to your party spirit?' he jeered softly. 'You turned it on for Duncan—how about some for me?'

'I didn't! Marc, *don't*!'

Her fists beat on his chest as he hauled her closer, his hands holding her hips and pulling her against him. 'Did you like it better when Duncan held you?' he demanded harshly. 'When he kissed you?'

Her nails dug into his arms, trying to shift them, and he grabbed at her wrists and twisted them behind her, pushing up her chin with his other hand. 'You weren't fighting him,' he said. 'You didn't scratch his face, beat bruises over his arms with your fists.'

'You don't understand—I didn't know how to stop him——'

'You didn't *want* to stop him, you mean. Just fooling around, was what you said.'

'It—it was! But that doesn't mean I wanted him to—

I just meant that you shouldn't be—angry about it. I didn't want you to hurt him.'

'That was your mistake, Kyla,' he said softly, his eyes holding hers. 'You should have let me hit him.'

Then his mouth came down hard on hers, and she realised with rising panic what he meant. The anger that he had not vented on Duncan was now all directed at her. His kiss was a savage punishment, his arms were a prison. When she moaned under his onslaught, he lifted his mouth for an instant, stared intently at her full, throbbing lips, and claimed them again with a hard, merciless passion.

After an age, his hand left her wrists to clamp on her waist, and she pushed feebly against his upper arms, but he only moved his hand from her throat about her shoulders, pushing her head into the curve of his arm as he went on kissing her without allowing her any respite from the cruel demands of his mouth.

Kyla went limp, and his grasp loosened. She wrenched away from him, running for the door, but he caught her before she got there, spinning her about with a tight grip on her shoulder, and pushing her against the wall, keeping her there with a hand beside her head and his body close against hers.

She saw the blaze of angry desire in his eyes and whispered, 'No, Marc! Please—not this way!'

His hand moved from her shoulder to grasp her throat, lightly but with a subtle menace in the strong fingers. 'You don't understand, Kyla,' he said almost gently. 'You don't have a choice any more. It's going to be this way—*my way*. I tried giving you time, I tried treating you gently, taking things a step at a time. And every time I got a slap in the face. My God, I even tried the platonic friendship bit, hoping you'd eventually learn to be able to give a little. But you only got colder, and further away from me. Well, not tonight.'

He was very close to her, and she was terribly aware of his body and its physical response to that closeness. 'You —promised . . .' she said, her voice choked.

'I think you know damn well that promise had to depend on some co-operation from you. You haven't kept your part—you can't expect me to feel bound by that.'

'I tried, Marc—I did try!'

His mouth was bitter. 'Then it wasn't much of a try, was it?'

His hand moved again, cupped her breast firmly, his fingers kneading its softness, and Kyla gasped and moved her head aside in despair.

'You'll learn to like it,' he said roughly.

Her mouth trembled. 'It hurts,' she whispered.

He took his hand away, moving a little so that he wasn't pressing quite so closely against her. 'I'll kiss it better,' he said softly, and his hands went behind her and she felt the zipper of her dress sliding down.

'*No!*' she cried. Her hand flew up, and as he grabbed at it, close to his face, she bent her head and bit his wrist. He cursed and pulled back, but her brief bid for freedom was quickly foiled as he slammed an arm hard about her waist, pulling her back against him. She felt his fingers pulling at the pins in her hair, then he had a handful of it and her neck was bent painfully as he turned her head until her mouth met his savage kiss.

His hands wrenched her dress away from her shoulders, and when she tried to stop him he was rough with her. He released her mouth as the dress slid to the floor at her feet, and swung her struggling body up in his arms, striding across the passageway to the dim bedroom. 'Some women only like it this way,' he muttered thickly. 'I'm beginning to think you're one of them.'

'*I'm not!* she almost shrieked at him. 'Don't *dare* to say that, you *beast!*'

He laughed briefly. 'Always so ladylike,' he mocked. 'Can't you think of anything worse than that to call me?'

'Bastard!' she panted, trying to hit out at him as he laid her down on the bed.

'Remind me to teach you some real swear words some time,' he said as he almost negligently fended her off, catching her wrists as he lowered himself beside her, throwing his leg across hers to keep her still.

Her brief half-slip had ridden up to her thighs, and she saw his glance flicker over her slim legs, then move slowly to her bare midriff, and linger on the shadowed valley between the lace cups of her bra. When he moved a hand to the waistband of her slip, she began to fight him desperately, and it took him several minutes before he succeeded in removing it. She was lashing out with hands and feet, and he concentrated then for a while on getting her under control. Her wrists were pinned above her head by one of his hands, and his bent leg across her thighs pressed warmly on her skin, holding her legs down. For a few seconds she writhed under him, trying to throw him off and get away from him, but it dawned on her that the frantic movements of her body only excited him, and she went still and began to shiver in sheer terror.

The light was very dim, and when Marc moved his hand she didn't at first realise what he was doing. Then she saw that he was unbuttoning his shirt, and when his hand went to the buckle on his belt, she heard her own voice pleading with him, and at the same time she began to struggle again.

He stopped her voice with his mouth, not as brutal this time, but moving on hers with sensual persuasion. Her wrists were still imprisoned by one of his hands, but the other moved lightly over her skin, trying to soothe her out of her blind, frantic fear. She moaned protestingly, and gradually stopped her fierce, futile movements of rejection.

When he lifted his mouth from hers, she was panting, exhausted and frightened.

Marc's head went down on the pillow beside hers, his voice low in her ear. She felt the searing heat of his body against her skin, and his breath was quickened and harsh. 'I'm not going to stop this time, Kyla,' he muttered. 'Don't fight me any more. Let me make it love—let me show you how good it can be—I don't want to hurt you.'

But as his hands relaxed a little, all she could think of was escape, and she made a desperate, convulsive movement of her body, arching away from him, trying to slide out from the weight of his thighs and chest.

He slammed her back against the bed, looming over her threateningly.

His voice harsh, he said, 'All right. God knows it shouldn't be like this when it's your first time with a man, but this time we're going to follow through—all the way, Kyla, and no turning back, no slammed doors, no last-minute slaps in the face.'

'So that you can prove what a *man* you are?' she cried bitterly. 'You don't need to worry, Marc—you're not the first. You can't hurt me, the way you mean—other ways, yes. But not—not *that way*!'

'What do you mean?' he demanded. His hands hurt her, and his eyes gleamed in the gathering dark as he tried to see her face.

'What I said,' she told him in a tired, husky whisper. 'You're not the first.'

She felt his shock in the utter stillness of his body; he didn't even seem to be breathing.

'You bloody little liar!' he muttered finally, his voice rough with anger.

'That isn't fair!' she said in a low voice. 'I never lied to you.'

'What else would you call it? That's why you wouldn't

let me near you, isn't it? You were afraid I'd know.'

'Yes,' she admitted tiredly, 'I suppose that was part of it.'

He suddenly released her, swinging his feet to the floor, sitting on the side of the bed, while he raked a hand through his hair. 'Why didn't you tell me?' he muttered.

'You made it rather difficult,' she told him unsteadily. 'You were so sure you knew all about me. Are you feeling cheated?'

'Cheated? I suppose so. I thought—you know what I thought.'

'Yes. I'm s-sorry—that I'm n-not——'

He turned to look at her. 'Are you crying?'

Kyla shook her head, unable to answer him, trying to drag the cover of the bed over her. She was shivering uncontrollably, her teeth chattering. Reaction.

Marc switched on the bedside light and stood up, appalled at the sight of the shudders racking her.

'What is it?' he said sharply. He grabbed at her robe that was hanging over the foot of the bed, and put it around her, helping her slide her arms into it.

'I'll be all right soon,' she gasped, still shivering as he hauled at the blankets and drew them up over her.

He took one of her hands and began rubbing it, but she pulled sharply away. Marc's jaw tightened, and he said, 'I'll get you a drink.'

'Something hot—please,' she said. He looked back from the doorway, and went out. He made her have a small brandy first, while he boiled up the kettle for tea. The brandy steadied her, and by the time the tea was drunk, she had stopped shivering altogether.

Marc took the cup and stood looking down at her, with a frown between his eyes, but she looked away, her fingers tense on the sheet.

'Do you want to sleep?' he asked abruptly.

She nodded her head because she wanted to be left alone, not because she thought sleep was possible.

He reached to switch off the lamp, and she said sharply, 'Leave it on! Please.'

Marc straightened slowly. 'All right,' he said, and went out, closing the door.

Kyla had thought she wanted to cry, but no tears came. She had the odd sensation of being in some sort of vacuum. Her emotions seemed temporarily dead, for she felt nothing. She would have to talk to Marc, he was entitled to a proper explanation. It was something she knew she should have done months ago. Now it might be too late. It was strange that she could think about that possibility with detachment. The only trouble was, the comfortable emotional anaesthesia couldn't last.

Surprisingly, she dozed for a time, her mind troubled with half-dreaming images from the past. She woke suddenly and completely to a silent house, so silent she wondered if Marc had gone out, or perhaps gone to bed in the other room. It was only ten-thirty. She felt it was going to be a long night.

She realised her hair was spread out in tangled strands against the pillow, and stumbled out of the bed, going to the dressing table for a brush and comb. She pulled the brush through her hair fiercely, until it was smooth and tidy, and tied it back off her face with a ribbon, then straightened the gown she wore and quietly opened the bedroom door and made her way to the bathroom.

When she came out again she went into the kitchen, looked for a packet of cocoa and opened the refrigerator for some milk to heat. She was turning with the jug in her hand when Marc appeared in the doorway from the dining room.

Kyla jumped, her sudden movement catching the jug

on the refrigerator door, and knocking it from her hand.

Milk splashed her bare feet, and Marc rapped out, '*Don't move!*'

He took a hand towel from the rail by the door and dropped it over the mess of milk, bent to pick up the pieces of the jug that lay jaggedly about her feet, and put them on the bench.

Kyla carefully stepped over the towel and stopped to pick it up. Marc's hand on her arm stopped her, pulled her back, and placed her firmly into a chair by the table. 'I'll do it,' he said.

He cleaned it up quite quickly, and as he rinsed out the towel at the sink, she said, 'I thought you were in bed.'

'Why?'

'There were no lights.'

He looked round at her briefly. 'I've been sitting in the dark. It's easier to think, that way.'

'I—have to talk to you,' she said.

'Yes.' He put down the wet towel, and turned to look at her. 'Were you going to have a drink of milk?' he asked.

'Cocoa. I meant to make some cocoa.' She picked up the packet off the table and started to rise.

'I'll make it,' he said, and took the packet from her hand. He found an unopened bottle of milk and a saucepan, and Kyla sat clasping and unclasping her fingers together on the table while she watched him make the drink.

'Aren't you having anything?' she asked as he placed the steaming cup in front of her.

He shook his head, pulled out a chair and then seemed to change his mind. He moved about the room, and as she took the cup in two hands to raise it to her lips, he swung round. Kyla's hands trembled and a little of the hot liquid spilled before she gulped some down. She put the cup back on its saucer with a small clatter, and glanced up at him.

Quietly he said, 'You knew what I thought.'

Her throat hurt as she whispered, 'Yes, I knew.' She looked away again and her mouth took on a bitter line.

Marc made an impatient gesture. 'It wouldn't have mattered—if you'd been honest. A man hardly expects a virgin bride these days. But you put up such a show of innocence and inexperience. Why the deceit?'

'It wasn't deliberate,' she said. 'You took too much for granted. If you'd ever asked, I'd have told you.'

'Would you?' His voice held cynical disbelief. 'But you made sure I wouldn't ask, didn't you? You pretended you didn't even know how to kiss . . .'

She winced. 'It was true.' Her voice rose a little. 'I wasn't putting on an act. I told you, I haven't lied to you, Marc.'

'You just withheld the truth.'

'Some of it . . .'

'You said that you'd never had a love affair.' He came closer to the table. 'But I can't imagine you giving yourself lightly—without love.'

She looked up then in quick hope, because his voice had softened a little. He was looking at her with puzzled speculation. 'What happened?' he asked. 'A single lapse of self-control? A night when you drank more than you could handle, and got into a situation you couldn't get out of? Or a teenage party that got a bit out of hand? Is that why you were ashamed to tell me?'

Kyla shook her head. 'You're quite wrong. It was nothing like that.'

'Then tell me!' He leaned across the table, his voice forceful. 'You just said you would have told me if I'd asked. I'm asking now. *Who was he?*'

She looked up at him with a bitter smile and said mockingly, '*He?*'

For a moment his eyes were blank with shock. Then he straightened suddenly and said softly, 'Oh, God!'

Turning away, he walked several paces before he faced her again. 'Well?' His face was expressionless and hard as he waited for her to go on.

Kyla took a deep breath, and trying not to think, began to tell him.

She told him about the small country town she had been brought up in. 'One of those places where everyone knows everyone else, and half the population is related in some way. I was in the sixth form, studying for the University Entrance exam, when I was seventeen. Everyone thought I would pass. And I had a part-time job, just once a week, as an usherette at the local picture theatre—Saturday night, when they needed extra staff. Sometimes the manager took me home, but I usually walked. It wasn't far, and there were generally quite a lot of people about. There's not much crime in a place like that, no one thought it was—unsafe. One night it was raining, there hadn't been many people in the theatre because of the weather, and the manager couldn't start his car—some water had got into the engine, probably. He offered to walk home with me, but he lived in the opposite direction and I said I'd be all right. I was walking along the main street, and it started to really pour down, so I stayed under a shop veranda, waiting for it to ease off. And a car came along. I didn't know the driver, but he had two passengers. One was a boy I knew—he'd left school the year before, but until then he'd been in my class, I'd danced with him at school dances and local parties. The other boy was someone I'd seen about the district, although he left high school the year I started. When they offered me a lift home, I accepted. It wasn't like taking a ride from strangers.'

She was aware that Marc had gone very still, but she kept her eyes fixed on the table before her. Now that she had started, the story came more easily. She had thought herself back across the years into the mood that had helped her to face the terrible days when she had been forced to relate the events of that night in court, and her voice unconsciously assumed the flat, monotonous tone she had adopted then. She had already been over it again and again with the police and the prosecution lawyer. She tried to tell it as though she was reading from an old newspaper; the car continuing down the main road instead of turning into her street, her realisation that the young men had been drinking heavily, her protests, and then her panic-stricken pleas to be taken home, the sudden silence when the driver turned off the main road. And when they finally stopped, miles from the township, she had tried to get out and been pulled back roughly, had fought free and tried to run across the deserted quarry in the rain and the dark and the mud, knowing there was no escape for her, that it was only a matter of time before her pursuers caught her . . .

'*That's enough!*'

Marc's voice cracked across the room and stopped her, cutting off her voice and bringing her jarringly back to the present.

He said, 'I can guess the rest.' His voice sounded forced and harsh. Kyla still dared not look at him. She sat mute, a strange thudding sensation in her throat, her hands and forehead clammy with tension. Marc said, 'You should have told me. *My God!* Didn't you think I had a right to know?'

She looked up briefly, then, and saw what she had dreaded. His face was pale, and there was a tight look of fury about his mouth and a savage anger in his eyes. And something else—distaste, disgust.

She closed her eyes. 'I'm sorry,' she whispered. 'Of course you had a right. I know I should have told you.'

She had hoped he would say it didn't matter, that it didn't make any difference. But it did make a difference. Underneath his tough exterior Marc was a romantic. He had thought her untouched, innocent, and that was what had made him want her. Now he knew the sordid truth, and what she had always feared deep down was painfully evident. In trying to pretend that he would understand, she had been foolishly deluding herself. It was up to her to find a way out, for both of them.

She risked another fleeting glance at his face and found the anger had abated a little, but the other look was stronger, now, and it was unmistakable—in his eyes, in his mouth—a sick disgust.

'I suppose we could—could get an annulment,' she said hesitantly. 'But I don't know what—evidence is required. It might be—difficult, in the circumstances. But divorce is quite easy, now, isn't it? If we're willing to wait for a year or two, and—and live apart.'

Marc was so long in replying that she might have been goaded into looking at him again if she could have borne to see his expression.

'Is that what you want?' he asked at last.

Her heart cried out in anguish against it, but she knew it would be worse to know that he was standing by their marriage while he tried to hide the way he felt about her. It would be easier not to see that look in his eyes again.

'Yes,' she said dully, 'I think it would be best.'

There was another pause. Marc made a sudden movement, quickly stilled, and said, 'All right.' He sounded hard now, like the driving businessman who had antagonised her when they first met. 'I'll see a lawyer in the morning. You'll be free as soon as I can arrange it.'

CHAPTER NINE

KYLA moved into the little flat over the shop. It was as good a place as any, while she decided what to do with her life. Her first thought was to go away, sell up the shop and run as far from Marc and their disastrous relationship as possible. But running away was a repeating pattern in her life, a pattern she had been determined to break. She had run from the little town where everyone knew her, when she could no longer stand the stares, the whispered conversations, the pity and the curiosity. Some people had been kind and understanding—the minister who had come and talked to her, told her that she must not feel smirched, that her mother had been mistaken when in a thoughtless moment she had bewailed that her daughter could not be married in white, that she had no reason for shame; and the minister's son, about her own age, had actually asked her to go out with him. She thought his father had put him up to it, and refused. In any case, her feelings were still too raw to accept any invitations. One or two other boys had been interested in her, but the sly curiosity she saw in their eyes made her flesh creep. Most of the boys she knew avoided her, embarrassed to be seen near her.

She had failed the University Entrance examination, after all, her study programme completely disrupted by the emotional trauma of what had happened to her, followed by the ordeal of the court proceedings and a prolonged absence from school. And as soon as she turned eighteen she left home and went to Auckland, to live in a hostel and find work, serving in a shop.

For a long time she avoided the company of men, but

one of the girls she worked with had a brother who seemed kind and gentle, and rather shy. The family was strongly religious, and Kyla felt safe enough with him when he asked her out. He was a good man, and she knew he was in love with her before he asked her to marry him. She thought she might come to love him, in time. But first she had to tell him what had happened to her. Of course he was shocked; she had expected that. She had not expected embarrassment and unease, and before long an obvious regret that their relationship had progressed so far. When she told him she had decided against marriage, his relief was palpable. It taught her a bitter lesson.

When next she liked a man enough to go out with him, he was much more extroverted, a man who made her laugh and hid her lack of confidence with his own ebullience. She wouldn't let him make love to her, and he was intrigued. When he seemed to be getting serious, she decided it was only fair to tell him her story before he got to the point of proposing. To her relief he seemed to accept it sympathetically; he held her hand and began asking questions in quiet tones, and she was grateful until the trend of the questions began to make her uneasy. She looked into his face and saw the eager, prurient interest in his eyes, and ran from him feeling sick and frightened and disorientated.

After that she grew a shell of outward poise and calm, cut men out of her life altogether, and, taking her savings, moved North to start her own business.

It was a pity that she had allowed Marc to get under her carefully built defences. A pity she had been stupid enough to persuade herself that if she didn't mention the past, it would not catch up with her.

No, she was not going to run away again. It wouldn't be easy, staying here where she might see Marc at any time. But she hoped it was not going to be easy for him, either.

The fault might have been mainly hers, but she couldn't quell an angry bitterness because he had not been able to understand, after all. If only he had loved *her*, and not the false image of her he had built in his own mind, her revelations would not have ended their marriage. Sometimes she hated him for that. There were moments when she found herself shaking with impotent anger, because he had made her love him, and his own love for her had been so easily withdrawn—and so cruelly.

Hazel had accepted her brief explanation that the marriage had not worked out with surprise and quickly hidden disapproval. Kyla could see her suppressing comment on the grounds that it was not her business, and was grateful that Hazel restrained herself from saying anything, other than a brief commiseration.

Marc was as good as his word, and a set of papers to be signed—the first step towards a divorce—arrived in the mail within a surprisingly short time. He wasn't wasting any time in getting rid of her, she thought with bitter pain.

Winter in the 'winterless North' was never really cold, but there were times when the winds blew chill, and days of rain coming down in torrents. Sometimes a day that started fine and warm would be dimmed by black, bloated clouds rolling over the harbour and on to the hills, suddenly spilling several inches of rain in a short time, before the sun emerged to set the pavements gently steaming.

On one of those days, Kyla slipped on the back step of the shop as she went out to close the door to the play area and stop the sudden rain from drenching some of the stock. Her ankle twisted painfully, and swelled a little, but although she limped for the rest of the day, she would not allow Hazel to stay later than her usual finishing time, so that she could see a doctor.

'It's nothing,' she insisted. 'I only twisted it.'

'Well, at least let me put a good firm bandage on it before I go,' Hazel insisted. 'You're limping badly. If I wasn't going to Tauranga this weekend with the family for this wedding anniversary of Denny's parents, I'd insist on your coming home with me. Are you sure you can manage?'

'Quite sure. It's nothing, honestly.'

'I don't know. You went awfully pale, and I don't like that swelling. You be careful on those stairs.'

'I will. Now, do go home. I know you want to start travelling as soon as possible tonight.'

On Friday nights the shop was open until eight-thirty. Kyla closed five minutes early, thankful that the rain which had set in steadily over the last few hours had kept most people at home. Her ankle throbbed and she felt faintly sick and a little dizzy. She went painfully up the stairs to the flat, which seemed bleak and lonely, and made herself a hot drink. After she had drunk it she sat in the one armchair, tiredly contemplating the empty cup. Her ankle was almost comfortable now that she had taken the weight off it, and she felt too exhausted to move again. She listened to the rain, and was passionately glad that she was safe and warm inside, not out there getting cold and wet. As a child she had liked the rain, but now it brought back too unpleasant a memory.

But she wouldn't think about that. She tipped her head back and closed her eyes. Just for a few minutes ...

A sound other than the rain penetrated her consciousness, and she realised that she must have dozed off in the chair, for almost an hour and a half had passed since she came upstairs. She would have to move, get undressed and go to bed.

But the sound came again, a pitiful, despairing yowl from outside. There was a family of kittens next door, offspring of a cat kept in a warehouse to keep the mice down. Stiffly, Kyla got up and went to the window. The blackness outside showed her nothing, but the sound went on, a feline cry for help that she couldn't ignore.

She found a torch and went down the stairs, holding hard to the banisters to take the weight off her injured ankle. She opened the back door, flashed the torch about the yard, and called, 'Puss, puss, puss?'

The kitten answered with a heartrending cry, and the torch beam located it clinging, wet and miserable, to a branch high up in the single tree.

Kyla hesitated. Her raincoat was upstairs; in her sleepy haste she hadn't thought of bringing it down. And in a shirtwaisted wool dress, she was hardly dressed for climbing trees.

But the rain had stopped at the moment, and it shouldn't be difficult to reach the kitten by way of the short ladder to the tree house. She couldn't face going all the way up the stairs again on her sore ankle to get a raincoat or a change of clothes.

She limped out into the night, skirting the patch below the tree house and the swing, where the children's feet had worn away the grass and the rain had created a muddy patch. Carefully she went up the ladder and stood on the platform at the top, trying to coax the kitten down. It took some time, and the rain began to fall again. Kyla had to inch up further than the tree house, trying to use her good foot to take her weight, and twigs caught at her hair, loosening the pins until strands fell into her eyes. She reached for the terrified little animal, felt her dress tear on something, and her fingers clutched at wet fur.

Ungratefully, the kitten struggled all the way down, scratching her hand and leaping to the ground as they reached the ladder, to streak away under the fence. Kyla dropped the torch in an effort to keep her balance as the kitten's sharp little claws raked her arm in its flight, and she heard a man's shout as her foot slipped on the ladder and she went flying down the last few feet to land on her side and her hands in the patch of mud at the foot. The voice yelled again as the slimy·feel of the mud made her skin crawl with revulsion, and she looked up to see a male figure outlined in the light from the doorway, running to-towards her.

She screamed, stumbling as she tried to get to her feet, to turn and run, screamed again when her ankle turned under her. She clawed at the ladder, dragged herself up-right, and as the rain came down hard, pelting her shoulders, she turned like an animal at bay. Her face, as he picked up the fallen torch and flashed the light over her, was a mask of nightmare terror.

Immediately he turned the light back to himself. 'Kyla!' She heard his voice before she realised the face was Marc's, pale and terribly taut, his mouth tight with some emotion fiercely controlled, his eyes looking almost black and strangely anguished. The rain had wet his hair, and rivulets of water were running down his face. He dashed a hand across his eyes, and Kyla had the fantastic idea that the moisture on his cheeks was something other than rain. Then he turned the light down to the ground between them, and said in a voice that was shaking a little, 'Kyla, don't run from me, *please* don't. I'll never hurt you, never again. I promise, darling. I promise.'

She didn't move, still pressed against the ladder. Her ankle was hurting abominably, now, and she felt the rain soaking through her clothes, plastering her bedraggled hair to her face. She could feel mud sticking to her fingers. She was fighting down hysteria, afraid to let go her grip on the ladder, her grip on herself. Her teeth clenched tightly together, the taut muscles of her arms quivered.

Marc went on talking, and she hardly heard the words, only the low, soothing tones of his voice, and realised that he was trying to coax her out of her fear, as she had done with the kitten.

She must move, she *must*. She couldn't stay here shivering in the rain all night, and Marc—Marc, she realised dimly, was afraid to touch her. She slowly released her grip on the ladder, pushing herself upright. She stood on her good foot, and Marc stopped talking, his stance suddenly alert. She tried her other foot, swayed, and righted herself. Marc shot out a hand, moved forward, then quickly withdrew without touching her.

Kyla slowly stretched out her hand. 'Marc—help me, please ...'

He let out a sudden, explosive breath, and picked her up in his arms, cradling her with gentle strength against his chest. He carried her in silence into the building and up the stairs to the flat, put her on her feet, still supporting her, and pushed the wet hair from her eyes with his fingers.

Her voice wobbling, she muttered, 'I'm a mess—I want to get clean——'

'I know,' he said, his voice still soothing, 'I know. If I help you into the bathroom, will you be able to manage? What do you want to put on?'

He found her warm, soft dressing gown for her and turned on the shower before he left her in the bathroom. Kyla washed her hair under the shower and wrapped it in a towel before she emerged from the bathroom, holding on to the door frame to steady herself. She had discarded the muddied bandage, and her foot hurt.

Marc must have been waiting for her. He turned from the heater that he had switched on, and she realised that he had hung his wet shirt over a chair, to dry in front of the electric bar. His bare chest was brown and had a slight covering of dark hair down the middle.

He took two steps towards her, and stopped. 'Shall I put my shirt on?'

Kyla realised she had been staring. 'No, of course not,' she said with an effort. 'It's wet.'

He came on, then, hooked an arm about her waist and said, 'Lean on me.'

He had turned the armchair to face the heater, and although he didn't seem cold, she was grateful for the warmth. Marc put her into it, and squatted in front of her, lifting the twisted ankle on to his knee. 'Where's your first aid stuff?' he asked. She told him, and he fetched an elastic bandage and bound it firmly. 'Better?' he asked as he straightened up, looking down at her.

'Yes. Thank you.' She saw that his trousers were steaming a little as he stood in front of the heater. 'I—didn't recognise you out there,' she said. 'I didn't know it was you.'

For a moment there was silence. Then he said, 'Would your reaction have been any different, if you had?'

Shocked, she looked up at his face, seeing it darkly bitter. 'Of course it would,' she said. 'I'm sorry I screamed. I was frightened.'

'Yes. At least I've never made you scream before.'

She didn't know what to say to that. She looked at his shirt, smeared with mud that must have come from her hands or clothes, and still wet. She asked, 'Why are you here—and how did you get in?'

'Hazel was worried about you. She rang me, said you had hurt yourself today, and she had been trying to phone you without getting any reply. She was afraid you might have fallen down the stairs or something. I told her I'd come down and check. You left the spare key at the house, remember.'

'Oh. Yes—I'd forgotten about it.'

'I did knock when I arrived, but when there was no

response I used the key. What on earth were you doing climbing trees at this time of night?'

She told him about the kitten, and he smiled slightly. 'And you can't stand getting wet and muddy and untidy,' he commented.

'I couldn't leave the poor thing. I expect you felt the same about me, when Hazel rang.'

His eyebrows rose a fraction. 'Not quite, I think.' He added, 'Why didn't you answer your phone?'

'I didn't hear it. Maybe it's out of order. I did doze off for a while, but not so heavily that I wouldn't have heard it.'

'Well, you'd better get hold of the telephone repair service in the morning.'

'Yes, I will. Thank you for coming. It was kind of you.'

'Are you throwing me out?' he asked.

'I didn't mean it like that. But I expect you'd like to get away.'

'If you want to get rid of me, there's no need to be so polite about it.'

He picked up his shirt from the chair, and Kyla protested, 'I don't *want* you to go! Your shirt isn't even dry yet.'

Marc paused with the shirt in his hand. 'I'd like to think you meant that.'

She thought of her first glimpse of his face tonight, and the words which she had barely heard at the time, and she said, 'I meant it. Please dry your shirt. Didn't you have a coat?'

'I didn't stop for one.'

He wasn't looking at her, but draping his shirt back over the chair, taking rather unnecessary care. 'Are you lonely here? Do you get nervous on your own?'

I'll be lonely for the rest of my life, she thought. Aloud, she said, 'It isn't so bad. I've got used to it.'

'So quickly?' He turned to look at her. 'You adapt faster than I do. I—haven't got used to being without you.'

That was unfair. 'I expect you will,' she said huskily. To avoid his eyes, she pulled the towel from her hair and pensively felt the damp ends. They didn't drip, and she made a move to get up.

'What do you want?' Marc asked.

'My brush and comb.'

'Where are they?'

'In the bathroom.' She sank back as he strode over to the bathroom door, returning to place them in her lap. He took the damp towel from her shoulders and dropped a dry one about them. Kyla picked up the comb and as she raised her hand the sleeve of her gown fell back to the elbow. Marc suddenly dropped the damp towel he was holding and shot out a hand to grasp her wrist, looking at the long red scratch marks on her arm.

'The cat,' she explained. 'It was frightened, and it scratched me.'

'Yes, of course,' he said on a strange note. 'You'd understand that, wouldn't you?'

Her eyes went to his neck, where she had scratched him once when he frightened her, and she felt a faint burning in her cheeks. He was still holding her wrist, and suddenly he went down on his haunches beside the chair and put his lips to the raw, red marks on her inner arm.

The subsequent shock of pleasure startled her, and she instinctively pulled away. Marc's hand grabbed hard at the arm of the chair to steady himself. With his head bent, he muttered, 'I'm sorry.' Then he stood up abruptly and moved away, his expression tight, putting out his hand to the still faintly steaming shirt by the heater to feel the fabric. His hand was shaking a little, and he snatched it back and thrust it into his pocket.

Kyla began slowly combing out her hair, watching him.

His head was turned from her, the muscles taut under the brown skin of his torso. A sensation that was utterly strange to her began to course through her body. For the first time in her life she felt a stirring of specifically sexual desire, and it bewildered her.

Her hand went on automatically wielding the comb until her hair lay smooth and straight against her shoulders. Marc hadn't moved, but he must have been aware of her movements, because when she put down the comb he looked at her and said, 'You haven't used the brush.'

'I usually brush it dry in the sun.'

'There's no sun. Won't the heater do?'

'I suppose so.'

He said, 'Come on, then.' His hands pulled her gently from the chair, and he took a cushion from it, dropping it in front of the heater, not too close, and settled her on it.

He half lay on the carpet beside her, propped on his elbow and watching the rhythmic movements of her arm. Selfconsciously, Kyla kept her eyes cast down, and went on brushing until her arm was tired, and the ends of her hair were curling slightly as it dried. She put the brush down and said, 'I should tie it back.'

'Please don't,' Marc said quietly. 'It's beautiful like that.'

Kyla clasped her hands tightly in her lap.

Inwardly trembling, she sat like a statue. Outside the wind was rising, and when the windows rattled to a whistling, moaning gust, she looked up apprehensively, her eyes wide and dark.

Marc said, 'Shall I stay with you tonight?'

She knew he didn't mean to sleep with her. He thought she was nervous, and was offering his protection.

'Wouldn't that delay our divorce?' she asked him.

'Not the way I meant it.'

'I know what you meant,' she said.

'Are you in a hurry to be free?' he asked.

'Don't, please, Marc!' She made a hasty movement to stand up, and he moved quickly to help her, his hands on her arms lifting her to her feet. He moved his hands down to hers and held them.

'*Are* you in a hurry?' he repeated.

Her fingers moved nervously in his. 'There's no sense in prolonging it,' she said. 'We might as well get it over with.'

His hands tightened for a moment, and then he released her. 'If that's what you want.'

His voice sounded curt and Kyla felt a spark of annoyance. 'It's what *you* want!' she said crossly.

'I never asked you for a divorce,' he reminded her angrily. '*You* suggested it.'

'And you were glad enough to take me up on it!' she retorted. Suddenly they were glaring at each other, tempers flaring so quickly she could hardly believe that only moments ago they had been sharing a quiet, poignant companionship.

'*Glad?*' Marc was frowning fiercely in disbelief. 'What the hell are you talking about?'

'Relieved, then,' Kyla shrugged. 'What's the difference? You wanted an end to our marriage as much as I did.'

Harshly, he said, 'You admit you want it ended, then?'

'Yes. I couldn't stand to—I couldn't bear——'

'All right, I know.'

She looked up at him miserably, and said, 'Do you, Marc? I find that very hard to believe.' Her temper died, and his face looked less harsh.

'Would it make a difference if I gave you my word I won't touch you again—unless you want it?' he asked in a low voice. 'I swear it—and I'm making no conditions, *nothing* will be expected of you.'

'What do you mean?' she asked in a whisper.

'I'm asking you for another chance. I never wanted a

divorce—dammit, you must have known that! I want you back. I promise you it will be different, this time. Now that I know——'

Kyla flinched and turned away.

'I don't understand,' she said. 'You don't want me. Why should you want to continue with a marriage that's— that can't be real?'

'I want you, Kyla, don't mistake that. I want you very much, in every way. I don't look forward to a *platonic* marriage. But if it's all you can take, I'll settle for that. It's only fair to tell you that I intend it to be real, in time. But only when you feel able to accept my wanting you—in that way, as well as all the other ways.'

'But——' her voice shook, 'how can you—when you despise me—when I disgust you——?'

There was a thunderstruck silence. Then hard hands dragged at her shoulders, turned her to face him, and she saw a strange mixture of fury and incredulity in the dark eyes blazing into hers.

'Will you tell me,' said Marc in an oddly unsteady voice, 'where *in hell* you got that idea?'

'I—*you*!' she stammered. 'When I told you about— about what happened to me.' Her voice turning bitter, she said, 'First you talked about your *rights*, as though that was what mattered most. And then—you were so angry and—and so disgusted.' Her voice rose a little. 'Don't deny it, Marc. I saw it in your face.'

His frowning eyes went blank. Then he said slowly, 'Oh —my—*God!*' His hands moved from her shoulders, and hovered as though he meant to put his arms about her and pull her close. Then he dropped them and turned swiftly away, one hand pushing through his dark hair and then kneading the back of his neck. 'Must I add *that* to everything else I've done to you?' he muttered raggedly. Then he swung round to face her, his feet planted apart on the carpet, his thumbs hooked into his belt.

'Listen to me,' he said. 'When you told me what had happened to you, I felt—violent. I wanted to track them down and smash them with my bare hands, for what they'd done to you. And then—it dawned on me that I'd just damn near raped you myself and that made me about on a level with them. I was disgusted, all right—sick with it. But never with you. I despised *myself*, Kyla, not you! When I said—I had a right to know, I only meant that if you'd told me before, I would never have tried to force you—I would have understood. I should have guessed, of course. The signs were there if only I hadn't been such a blind, arrogant fool. I didn't blame you for wanting to be free of me.'

'But, Marc, it was only because I thought you didn't want me—and I couldn't stand the look on your face, when I thought it was directed at me.'

He shook his head as though that baffled him. 'I thought you couldn't stand having me near you. I'd been a greedy, selfish and stupid brute to you——'

'You weren't!'

'Yes, I was. I rushed you into marriage, made inane assumptions about you—and even if they'd been right, I should have had some patience. Instead, I got furious when I failed to turn you on—perhaps deep down I had some crazy notion that it reflected on my manhood. You accused me of that ... And when Duncan kissed you, and you didn't fight like the little wildcat I knew you could be, I reacted like a savage—behaved like *them* ...'

'*No!* It wasn't the same, Marc. It wasn't!'

'Your feelings were the same, though, weren't they?' he said quietly. His mouth twisted suddenly. 'Oh, *God*, Kyla! When you ran from me tonight, I wanted to die—to kill myself—for making you so frightened.'

She saw the same look of anguish in his eyes she had

seen then, and whispered, 'Oh, Marc, *no*!' She took a step towards him, stretching out her hand in protest. She saw his mouth clamp tight, and the waiting, hoping look in his eyes.

'I wouldn't have run from you,' she said. 'I didn't know it was you.'

Marc didn't move or speak, but his eyes asked her to prove it. She had never been the one to make the first move, but this time she must. She took a halting step, and his hands left his belt, falling to his sides.

His eyes still held hers as she went to him and slid her arms about his bare waist. His hands were clenched by his sides, and it was a moment before they lifted and folded her close to him with infinite gentleness. She felt his chest rise and fall against her cheek, and after a few minutes she rubbed her face against his bare skin.

'Kitten,' he murmured. 'You shouldn't do that.'

'Why not?' She moved her hands, stroking the warmth of his back, her fingers finding the line of his spine. 'I like it,' she said, surprised at the smoothness of his skin under her fingers. She moved her face against him once more, then turned her head a little and pressed a soft kiss against his shoulder.

She felt him go still and rigid. 'So do I,' he said, and suddenly moved, gripping her upper arms and holding her away. 'Too much.'

Deliberately, Kyla put her hands against his chest. His heart beat strongly against her fingers, and she felt a slight dampness under them. 'I never wanted a divorce,' she said. 'Never. I want a marriage.'

Marc bent his head and kissed her briefly. 'Yes,' he said. 'It's more than I deserve, but God knows it's what I want, too.'

Kyla hooked her arms about his neck. 'Stay with me tonight, please, Marc.'

He looked at her frowningly. 'Do you mean that the way it sounds?'

Feeling carefree and remarkably confident, Kyla smiled at him, her head tipped back to watch his face. 'You know what I mean,' she said.

As though he couldn't quite believe it, he lowered his head slowly until his lips met hers, and took them in a sweet, seeking, tender kiss. His arms brought her closer to his body, and she clung, returning his kiss with innocent abandon.

He lifted his mouth at last, kissed her throat with a passion that set her heart thudding, and pulled away a little, his hands on her narrow waist, holding her before him. 'You don't have to do this,' he said. 'It doesn't have to be all at once. Not if you don't want it.'

Kyla, already delighting in new sensations she had scarcely known existed, put her forehead down against his chest and complained softly, 'Marc, you're very hard to seduce!'

'*The devil I am!*' She heard the soft, disbelieving laughter in his voice, and then he hauled her close, so close she knew it wasn't going to be difficult at all, and quivered with the knowledge. His hold slackened, and he said, 'Does it scare you, honey?'

She shook her head, but that wasn't enough for him. He lifted her chin with his hand. His eyes asked the question again, and she whispered, 'Not when it's you, Marc.'

He kissed her lips softly, and she took his hand and put it on her breast, murmuring against his mouth, 'You said I'd learn to like it.'

'You will,' he promised, before his kiss deepened and stopped her talking. His hands this time were gentle, touching hers sensuously, and her sigh of pleasure came into his mouth before his fingers slipped inside her gown and stroked her naked flesh, bringing it to a hot, singing excitement.

He lifted her and then she was lying on the softness of the carpet, with her head on the pillow he had placed for her. Her hair spread over it, and a silken strand fell across her cheek, clinging to her mouth. She had a brief, horrifying memory of hard hands pulling, hurting, shoving a handful of her own muddied long hair into her mouth to stop her screaming, and then Marc's fingers gently touched her cheek, pushing the hair away from her mouth, smoothing it back against the pillow. Erasing the memory. His face filled her vision and her mind, but he was hesitating, touching her lightly and without haste. 'Tell me if you want me to stop,' he said. Kyla shook her head, and he kissed her, his mouth exploring, asking, tasting hers as though her lips intoxicated him. She found the scent of his skin delighted her, and the merest touch of his hand could make her feverish with pleasure.

When he moved from her a little, she opened her eyes and blinked at the glittering fire in his, but this time she saw the tenderness behind the desire and didn't flinch from it.

'Shall I turn out the light?' he asked her.

'No! Not in the dark.'

'Okay, darling. Not in the dark.' His fingers stroked her cheek and his mouth was soft against her lips.

There was a brief moment of darkness later, when she realised that in spite of Marc's promise, it was too late to stop anything. She felt a sudden chill of fear, and willed her body not to mirror it, not to reject him. Then she felt the warmth of the arms that enfolded her, the body that had become a part of hers, and the love that made a physical act into a relationship that brought hearts, minds and emotions, everything that made them, Marc and Kyla, into a total, mysterious union.

And there was a sudden, almost unbearable, fantastic explosion of light and feeling that sent her soaring into a dimension she had never dreamed of, that almost frightened her with its intensity. From a great distance she heard Marc's voice saying, 'You're all right, my darling. You're all right.'

She came back to earth with her head against his shoulder, and his fingers stroking her tumbled hair back from her face. His eyes were anxious, and darkened by a faint frown. She smiled and put a finger between his brows to smooth the frown, moved it to his mouth, and outlined his lips until he caught it gently in his teeth. Kyla laughed, and Marc pulled her closer and said, 'We should be in bed.'

They slept together in one of the two single beds, their arms about each other. The wind howled outside and the rain flung itself against the windows, but when Marc put his hand on the switch of the bedside lamp and looked at her questioningly, she said, 'Switch it off.'

The room was plunged into blackness, but Marc had scooped her into his arms, and her head was against his shoulder. She smelled the salty male aroma of his skin, and knew the dark, the rain and the wind had lost their power to frighten her. With Marc, there would be no more darkness.

THE ART OF BATIK

Kyla, Daphne Clair's heroine, owns a crafts shop—and no crafts shop would be complete without batiks. Perhaps you've heard the term and wondered just what it means.

"Batik" is an Indonesian word that means "wax writing," a special technique by which fabrics are dyed with rich colors in various designs. Although remnants of batik have been found in Egyptian tombs, it is thought that the method first originated in India.

Like tie-dyeing, batik is known as a "resist" technique. This means that before a fabric is colored, some portions are prepared to resist the dye. In batik, molten wax is painted on the cloth wherever the dye is not desired. After dyeing, the wax is removed by melting it off with a hot iron onto sheets of absorbent paper. Each time a new color is applied to the fabric a different portion of the cloth is waxed. This way patterns are produced and colors can be overlaid with other colors. The result? Fabulously rich reds, blues, yellows and an infinite range of colors in between, set in myriad patterns and designs limited only by the imagination of the batik artist.

But the most characteristic aspect of batik is the "veining" that appears through the design. This is caused when the wax coating cracks during coloring, allowing the cloth to absorb thin lines of dye in the resist areas. It is the veining that gives batiked cloth unpredictable and often startling beauty.

Dutch sailors and traders introduced batik to the West several hundred years ago. Today batik is popular not only because it is beautiful, but also because it is a craft that can be easily performed in the home. In an age when so much is done by machine, it is little wonder that handcrafted batiked fabric, which represents the individuality of its maker, has become popular once again.

Take these
4 best-selling novels
FREE

That's right! FOUR first-rate Harlequin romance novels by four world renowned authors, FREE, as your introduction to the Harlequin Presents Subscription Plan. Be swept along by these FOUR exciting, poignant and sophisticated novels . . . . Travel to the Mediterranean island of Cyprus in **Anne Hampson**'s "Gates of Steel" . . . to Portugal for **Anne Mather**'s "Sweet Revenge" . . . to France and **Violet Winspear**'s "Devil in a Silver Room" . . . and the sprawling state of Texas for **Janet Dailey**'s "No Quarter Asked."

 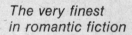

The very finest in romantic fiction

Join the millions of avid Harlequin readers all over the world who delight in the magic of a really exciting novel. EIGHT great NEW titles published EACH MONTH! Each month you will get to know exciting, interesting, true-to-life people . . . . You'll be swept to distant lands you've dreamed of visiting . . . . Intrigue, adventure, romance, and the destiny of many lives will thrill you through each Harlequin Presents novel.

Get all the latest books before they're sold out!
As a Harlequin subscriber you actually receive your personal copies of the latest Presents novels immediately after they come off the press, so you're sure of getting all 8 each month.

Cancel your subscription whenever you wish!
You don't have to buy any minimum number of books. Whenever you decide to stop your subscription just let us know and we'll cancel all further shipments.